THE ICE SCABBARD
Book 2

THE NIVIAN KING SERIES BOOKS

The Nivian King: Book 1
The Ice Scabbard: Book 2
The Arvinstrum: Book 3
The Army of Naquior: Book 4

SELECT NONFICTION

Persons Artificial
The Earth-Colonizing Handbook of Generation Stelan
God is DNA
The Science of Reality
Grand Robot
World War C

THE ICE SCABBARD
Book 2

PARIS TOSEN

Tosen Books

The Ice Scabbard: Book 2 is a work of fiction.

Copyright © 2011 by Paris Tosen

ISBN: 978-1-926949-21-5

www.tosen.ca

Book design and cover by Paris Tosen

THE ICE SCABBARD

Love as a cool evening breeze. — Nata

Chapter 1

CHANCE FOLLOWS change into the flamma that when not burned burns more brightly until it shines freely and wipes out the darkness that hides in the shadows between the immaterial and the supreme. The flesh may wither without touch. May drown without so much. But that is the trivial.

If all that was required was influence in order to be given new flesh then it could be said that places of influence could be found, and in finding such nodes endowed with said capabilities, the permutations that would follow could not be prevented, and though they may bring hardened sorrows; they would also brush brightly the tomorrows.

Change followed in the independent urba of Casus. The urba was close enough from the mainland to enable Seronian solidarity and far away enough to fertilize its own inventions. Casus was a gray hole that attracted simple and complex forms of data contained in the bodies and actions of all the inhabitants of the planet. It attracted, sometimes rejecting and mostly adopting, improved ways for doing things and in so doing the urba improved and convoluted itself and all those inside its unstructured bounds. If there was one place on Seranor that exuded optimism for an unknown future, then it could be found on the large island upon which Casus was situated.

Mareenth was so disgusted by the meretricious urba that instead of joy it brought her misery. Her adoring husband, Shev'la, paid special attention to his wife's needs though never fully satisfying the real ones she kept to herself. It was her past that always came back to haunt her as it did for everyone else. She was moved beyond irrationality by the end of the forty-ninth tios in the urba of her wild youth, caught in the web of her past and the eye of reprisal.

Given a choice she would have not returned, but Zorath gave them neither choice nor compromise. It was technology that saved the three of them. The prototype flashport device Tulai developed had propelled them through the sky as rays of invisible flamma and they had arrived excited and unbroken near the outskirts of the urba. Technology in Tulai's hands was reliable. It rarely failed and when it did the consequences were few. The inventor was conservative and cautious mixed with a rich curiosity for things. Above all, he was a true genius in creation though limited by his mortalized physical restrictions. An embodiment of the Kozotal.

They made the best of it and spoke little about the incident in fear of the Nivian tracing them by their displeasure. Soon after the three had grown comfortable in their new habitat, Shev'la had found work as a communications expert to design cipher communications for a no-name organization. At the time, he didn't ask too many questions of his confident young boss, Ira, a kozoty from the north who was born in wealth of all things and moved with impeccable precision and class in the physical and the verbal.

With the introduction of a Seronian monetary system 25 tios before, it was automatic that the influential attained great wealth from the start in the form of *zorn*, Seronian currency. Ira came from such influence.

The Zorn Disc, made into a flat ceramic disc, hexagonal in shape, was well received. Zorn, as it came to be referred to, was loaded with purchasing credits, in the form of embedded glyphs. Necessary food and beverages were made available cheap as possible so that none starved, as long as one had a zorn-stocked disc; other items such as equipment, armor, shelter, as well as gambling and prostitution could be purchased. Payment was automatically withdrawn after command passwords, that matched entan scent, were given. The scent of an entan was considered a stable piece of input data and could be used for identification purposes.

Salaries were gained for work and were deposited daily to facilitate spending habits and the adoption of new ideas. The simple zorn concept was adopted on a massive scale at rapid speed like a virus spreading to kill its prey. Casus, and other major urbas, grew unmanageable and so *Zoranta*, financial banks used to administer zorn and other wealth, were formed by new organizations, and had sprung up throughout major centers in recent months. And so began *mercanomics*: the management of monetary distribution and control, economics, and business. At about the same time, the *Numular Council* was opened in three main urbas to regulate business and monetary exchange. The main branch of the Numular Council was in Casus.

IRA ALWAYS carried a long black batier, unbothered by its nuisance no matter the occasion, that was fitted perfectly in an ornate scabbard on his left hip and with his family mark inscribed upon it. Magnetic colored clothes were coated with strange materials that made them glisten in the light and faded black in the dark. Shev'la admired this noble kozoty and despite their differences of stature they had grown close over time. The two always spoke of serious topics and Ira was impressed at Shev'la's ability to remain in conversation during the most intellectual of times. Ira grew up in the kozotian north and was raised to become a leader of the military; he was well trained in physical and arvic combat. The greatest cerbinds came from the north, from the milk of kozoty, as they had been the descendants of Kozotal from long ago. His family were experts in the development of hand-to-hand weapons, armor and had begun experimenting with military devices long before any others.

The Seronian Guard was the basic military unit dressed in dull white banded armor marked heavily with imperfections. They all carried long handled clavuses, batiers with a circular hacking piece on the end, and basic identification discs designed to succeed in their purpose, to protect and watch over Seranor; and so boldly wore the *Seronian Torq*, a circular pattern of white and black seragons dancing together. The torq was the mark of the planet. The bright blue sea background encircled by an interwoven pattern at its edge represented Aquanomicus and all things contained in it.

All urbas were fitted with various numbers of Guards who facilitated trouble-free living and protected lives when seriousness developed from irresponsibility. The Captains of the Guard were blessed with different characteristics; some were ventans, gray entans who preferred ora over opus, whose aim was to increase suffering and to stifle those that were not reasonable in their oratic eyes.

Ira's family also researched and developed surveillance equipment and secret communications technologies among other things and had taken on Shev'la for building coded communications into the newest surveillance systems. He took a liking to cryptography, working with communication codes, stimulated by his youthful interest in it while tinkering with his father's devices, and strangely enough many of the technologies he touched now were reminiscent of the ones his father developed many tios before.

New technologies had entered the main urbas and Casus was one to pick up and try all the latest devices. The most recent technological device was the verse command operated *tard*, a dual purpose identification, registration and communications disc about two centimeters thick and five centimeters in diameter cast in an octagonal shape with a white face and a crystal in its center. Tards were introduced 18 tios ago by *Technomicon*, one of three organizations connected to the Mercantile Bases, using the latest ceramic and flamma-based technology far more advanced than any previously created. Some ten percent of the ceramination – population of ceramic beings – of Casus, as well as a handful of other urbas, now were using tards to stay in communication. The Seronian Guard adopted a basic model to be used in their ranks.

Each fat disc was attuned to its user's scent and was practically unbreakable by normal means. Different versions of tards were around. Some were customized. The tard used photon transmissions, flamma radiation, to communicate with other tards. Users could see the image of the caller on the other side and had a clear voice pick-up even in bad weather conditions. Flamma was a superior carrier of information, a medium of untapped ability. The tards were charged by arvicity using a special type of rare ceramic called *ganium*. Small amounts had been found and its property was to store arvicity for a limited amount of time.

The photon signal was not very strong as the crystal was inferior in quality and the arvicity that was used was sub-optimal. The system was currently limited to urbas which used flamma magnifiers to boost the signals, but once underground, communications relied on voice. Seronians weren't so particular. They enjoyed the new form of communications and the *palpazines*, a medium speaking for Technomicon mostly, promised much more in the tios to come.

Tards were sold for Z500, a fair amount of zorn, that most entans did not mind to pay. Once purchased a user had unlimited use of the tard. Basic licensing fees were built into the selling price. Technomicon's strategy was simple: increase the use and proliferation of the tard and then later add supplementary services and functions. For example, the company had developed an improved image enhancer and was already working on a secret transmission wave for confidential discussions. This complemented the public wave that was accessible to all. More services and functions were in development. Ira was intimately involved in communications along with many other technologies and Shev'la found opportunity to learn about commercialized products versus research-based ones; He most enjoyed the military-level of communications technology and its cryptic applications.

IRA AND Shev'la met after six months when he, upset at the unstable and moody nature that had possessed Mareenth since their arrival became worse and entered a point of violence, left their residence to find some place to sooth his aching head unable to solve his deteriorating family situation. He walked along the clean urba streets, walking past hundreds of differently dressed Seronians. After following a couple of armored figures brandishing heavy weaponry he found they arrived at the *Ice Scabbard*, a tavern filled with the strikingly strange. Most probably all those seeking adventure and perhaps their unknown destiny.

He cared not where he went and became somewhat interested in a tavern full of odd-dressed lutos and lutas in search of their true identities. The tavern was tall and red with a big sign lit by flamma at the top reading "The Ice Scabbard" in common verse and a long empty red scabbard inlaid with false glyphs along it. A loud noise of ceramin talking and singing could be heard from a distance. He preferred this noise over returning home early to face the dread once again.

Once inside he ordered the most popular drink on the house, *primo*, a specially mixed juice of anaprimo and freshly prepared mystery ingredients that gave everyone who drank it a buzz they wouldn't forget for several hours.

He had had a couple of goblets of primo and now felt quite arvicified by its effects, nothing seemed to matter to him and all thoughts about Mareenth and his brother and mother drowned in the juice. His sight became a restful plane and his ears sharpened their volume.

Rumors of White Crusaders walking the land in search of arvic relics were spoken without whisper. This was the Ice Scabbard after all and whose members came here afraid of nothing except what had yet to come. Shev'la couldn't help but to listen intently, curious to know what Casus was about and more so to hear what was so important on entan's cerbinds. His own cerbind had already begun to wander into the primo zone and he caught only the briefest of conversations.

Behind him a fat luto yelled, "It's loaded with treasure and a suit of armor impervious to all attacks! We must go before all the land is frozen…" To his right side another table spoke less openly with a slight fear in the speaker's voice.

"One crusader laid open the land with a fell swoop of his black rader," said a sharply dressed luto with twin short batiers on his back while talking to a table of young adventurers eager to hear what he had to say. "It is said they are untouched by arvicity and might and there were thirteen…but one has disappeared…some say assassinated by Sarcophagi…" He looked around cautiously then seeing something lowered his voice back into a whisper.

By then the primo had taken effect on him and he lay back with his head looking at the tall ceiling while life was exaggerated in the center of the wildest urba he had ever been to. He wondered what path he was on now and when it was his turn to get off or maybe he was just getting on. It was impossible to know how one arrived. Plans were rarely adhered to. He laughed at his own imagination and as he rolled his head from side to side he caught the bright colors of a quiet kozoty, the one who would later reveal himself as Ira Levin.

The colorfully dressed kozoty sat in one corner of the tavern, sitting by himself and drinking a tall glass of a bluish liquid, probably *wanine*, a favoured elemental drink of the kozoty. He sat calmly and proudly drinking while his batier, long and black, lay across the table top partially unsheathed revealing the black rod, of exquisite design, underneath.

It was not long after that when four masked individuals entered the tavern, their long blue hair flowing behind their fast pace and long white cloaks. They headed directly towards the lone figure who did not move in anticipation, and seemed to be aware of their presence.

Four cloaked figures surrounded the table speaking some verse then moments before the first weapon was drawn, Ira grabbed his batier, twisted it around in a jerking motion until the scabbard flew at lightening speed piercing the first enemy with his hand still on his batier as the enemy fell over dead. A second movement from the black batier came after Ira flipped backwards head-first from his seat,

narrowly escaping the clavus that crashed the chair
he was sitting on, landing an arm's length away
from the next opponent as the batier easily severed
off the right arm of the enemy then the left leg at the
knee. Both strikes directly on the joints. Milk
gushed out. But by the time he repositioned himself
to strike the third opponent he was caught by a spell
from behind that held him fast in his tracks and he
couldn't move.

All those in the tavern stood and watched as they
always did, never interfering in what was not part of
their business, but Shev'la could not sit to watch
without reacting. He leapt from his seat exercising
his aerial acrobatics which had now lost some
technique from not using it for 20 tios; his batier
came spiking down on one of the opponents, not
before Ira was stabbed through the left chest from
the one mysterious figure behind him. Shev'la
finished his opponent harshly but quickly then
looked at the kozoty for a response. None was
expressed.

Shev'la could see the held-fast batiersman trying
to cast a spell. Another blue spell came out and
Shev'la pushed Ira out of danger's way. The figure
in the back revealed his face, a karul, blue all over,
as he prepared another spell which was broken by a
flying chair from Shev'la's kick. He then moved in
close to hand combat and batiers clashed on batiers.
Shev'la was badly mismatched and got hit several
times. Milk ran from his arms and legs and his
breath became shallow as he stood his ground
fighting for someone he had not met before only

knowing that it was wrong to strike down any being without good reason. Naivety at its worst. He now thought about how he had endangered his own life and had not considered the effects that it would have on Mareenth. He blamed it on the primo. The karul caught him at the neck without following through. He lowered his batier. The challenge was lost.

Gasping with each word, Shev'la said, "I'm·not· finished·yet."

"You must learn when you have lost, friend. This is not your fight. Will you die for it?" said Folomir.

"You·will·die·for·it," he said, jealous of his confidence and angry at his own weakness.

"Death is the best teacher it seems," replied the karul.

He lunged again swinging widely enough for the blue·haired foe to bring his batier for the final blow and in a surprising intervention, a black batier stopped it dead in its path.

"This is between you and me, Folomir. Fight me with honor so that you may die with it," said Ira then faced Folomir. Both had batiers drawn. A silence fell upon the entire tavern.

"It is not yours to keep, Levin," the Karul said.

"I've gotten used to having it around," said Ira, looking over the black batier in his hand. "It suits me. You will leave here or die from that which you had sought."

They faced each other in combat form for several moments before Folomir cast out a spell then moved at blinding speed with his batier. Ira dispelled the blue light that came at him and shifted the weight of his weapon in his hands. Batier against batier came together only once then a black haze cut twice through the karul first removing a hand and second, and lastly, the neck. Folomir's head flipped over many times then landed in a crunch onto the floor and as it landed the entire tavern, once again, erupted in joyous laughter and song as if nothing had ever happened. Shev'la started bandaging his wounds and in midst of it all, a hand thrust out a singular vial of liquid.

"This should do you," said Ira.

"What is it?" asked the winded warrior.

"It will heal you. Drink it. It is some of the finest."

Shev'la took it quickly, examined it, slowly opened it then drank all in one swallow while staring at his new friend.

"What is your name?" asked Ira.

"Khan. Shev'la Khan."

"Khan...I am Ira Levin of House Levin and I am indebted to your assistance and for protecting my life as strange as it is for I have never been outmatched, well, regardless...it is done. I hope that you are feeling better."

"Yes," Shev'la looked at his wounds and they had all healed completely. "All wounds are gone."

"Then I was right, one vial was enough."

"Levin, right?" Shev'la recalled the visit by an Amid Levin shortly before Ulaq was destroyed. His father paid the Levin no heed.

"Yes."

"I knew a Levin once, at least my father did."

"Who would that be?"

"Amid, Amid Levin."

Ira went temporarily stone-faced then cracked into a smile. "Of course. You met my father."

"I never personally met him."

"Unfortunate. He was a great kozoty."

"Was? But—"

"He was killed. Listen, now that we've lost everyone's attention let's sit and talk some more. I am curious to know why it is that you and I have met."

Ira and Shev'la, or Khan as Ira called him not bothering to pronounce the more complex part, talked for several hours and by the time they both left he had offered Shev'la a job to work as a cryptographer.

Chapter 2

THERE WAS never a dull moment with Mareenth
miserably unhappy of her stay making certain that
her husband also lived with her pain; and Tulai's
guilt-pushed research into the lost connection
between entans and Seranor served to compress the
weight of three sinking kols in the depths of regret.

Shev'la and Mareenth finally agreed to give birth
to a seed by the middle of the second tio. He hoped
that this would calm the situation long enough for
him to make new arrangements. Mareenth's cerbind
became occupied by her bulging chest as essence
accumulated for the seedling's germination.

Birthing on Seranor was a most painful
experience, not because of physical torment but

because a critical decision had to be made and executed by the pregnant luta. A decision to willingly give one limb, her arm, for her seedling.

Once enough essence had been generated in a luta's chest she was then to perform a most difficult task – sever her own right arm. The severed arm containing the pregnant essence from the luto, white and pure, would fall to the ground and after the first month would curl up and turn black. By the second month entan formations would start, all covered by an orange-yellow cast. The third month was the most pronounced. By then, a beige body with two arms, two legs and a roughly-formed head would settle and could be called a new, genderless seed.

Mareenth, compelled to reach a resolution, had removed her arm with a sharp lutium blade. Her arm, of course, was immediately replaced by the remaining essence in her body and took on the usual roughly-shaped appendage that would attune itself over the months. New mothers could easily be spotted by their crudely-shaped right arms. It was only the right arm that could bear a seed though there were stories of mothers birthing both arms at once.

She cared for her seed during those tender months and after a tio, Mareenth and Shev'la had recognized a luta. Their luta was named Cal'la, after his brother Calil. Mareenth, her arm renewed, didn't seem to be bothered by the name as she was more preoccupied by her beautiful seedling.

Time passed more quickly than before and Shev'la kept busy in his work and only occasionally met with

Ira who became increasingly preoccupied with
mysterious emergencies and rendezvous with
strange cloaked figures in the oddest of places. Old
technologies were refined and new devices came onto
the market. Tards soon were prominent
communication devices and all of Seranor was slowly
becoming obsessed with zorn. And in the midst of all
of this Mareenth's interest in Casus diminished and
deteriorated, soon enough the distractions from
Cal'la were reduced as he grew and the cries of
anguish came again to their family.

Tulai, slightly discolored from his excessive
research and more pacifistic in character as the tios
passed on, struck arvicity when he chanced upon a
secret and ancient theory by reversing and slightly
modifying his Anativical Theorem. The new process
opened the theory of creation that held the key to
keeping Seranor alive indefinitely. In his
exploration of Seranor's power he traced black arvic
veins of still arvicity, energy replaced by anti-energy,
on the planet that were progressing and predicted
that they may soon cause her to degenerate past a
point of survival. By his best estimations unfound
pools of still arvicity were located on the planet, a
definite sign of the onset of the dying state. He
named it *Arvichiosis*, so that all could remember
what was killing Seranor – the joining of ora and
opus creating a deadly mix. He communed with the
Seranivas who told him that someone had been
drawing huge reservoirs of arvicity, unlike ever
before, and using it in the central region over the
past 25 tios. Tulai was certain that Zorath was

using large amounts of energy to further his plans of domination. It was probably the reason why the three of them were alive. Zorath did not waste time on things that mattered the least. He told Shev'la about some of this who was not sure how to react with his family in the picture.

Deciding that he would need others to carry on his work, he chose to educate Seronians and to teach them how to save Seranor. He continued to work late nights and in the daytime went into the urba centers like Ceramin Square to give seminars and speeches about his ideas. As the tios continued to be counted, his presence became respected by a select group of Seronians and followers began to grow. There was fear that he too would start a cult-like following such as others had started but whose interests were purely for zorn and the taste of control over others such as the Cult of Glass. Members of this cult wore mechanisms, containing thin porcelan pieces in varying degrees of opacity, over their eyes and were convinced that such mechanisms could bring out the true self. But Tulai was not interested in zorn believing that the milk of a volunteer like himself was invaluable. His growing number of followers also believed this to be true.

SHEV'LA CONTINUED to study cryptography and followed his father around as he did seminars and teachings with his followers about the importance of being connected to Seranor and ways to save her. Sometimes he listened to his father but most times he worried about Mareenth. She had become sick with despair and he knew that he could no longer convince her to stay in a place she absolutely loathed. If not for her love for him she would have abandoned any other after the first month. Shev'la had also heard more stories of the white crusaders scouring the land and if his father's opinion was right then these were also connected to Zorath.

The mere mention of his name brought back tears of his youth and the death of Calil and the loss of his dear mother. But if indeed it was Zorath there would be importance in this matter so he decided to search out Ira. He found him talking with a short luto of average build with shoulder-length cropped hair and a protruding nose. A small package was handed to Ira and zorn was traded for it. The luto quietly disappeared into the crowd without a trace of his existence.

"Ira, I am glad to catch you, old friend," said Shev'la.

"Khan, you are well?" inquired Ira. "How is your work progressing?"

"I have tasted better days but I seek information, Ira, of the private kind."

"Yes, yes come into this cell."

They both entered a plain-walled cell with several cora couches inside and a round black table in the center. It was deathly silent inside and the brown walls added a touch of warmth to a rather empty place.

"There is much talk these days of white crusaders—" started Shev'la.

"Ah, sooner or later I was sure to hear this from you," said Ira, remarking right away at the topic. Ira was one of the most well-informed Seronians on the planet.

"Do you know about them?"

"I have never met them."

"What are they?"

"I do not know so clearly at this moment but I know of danger, Khan. All the Houses are aware of them. House Draconus is most concerned while we have already been preparing for some time."

"Preparing for what?"

"It was inevitable that after two thousand tios of peace on the planet that something would come to eradicate what we have earned. You yourself may be aware of things. It is opus and ora all over again. Their battle will last for all days yet to come."

"There are truly crusaders then?"

"Yes, but more powerful than their stories do them justice. All of them – save one – wear the same white plate armor with a black rader, one ring, and a red helm with a black face that even the brightest flamma cannot penetrate."

"His servants have come," said Shev'la, recalling Anativo and his awakening.

"Then you know," replied Ira.

"Only of the Nivian King—Zorath."

"There is more," he started, not surprised of Khan's knowledge. "Zorath's power replicates by the day stealing Seranor's secrets from the Seranivas and Niva, the ice spirit, and has decided to begin a movement to usurp all the power in Seranor and to cast it back at those that betrayed him on Nivata. My House has been following his movements from the time he unleashed the power of an ancient device on the land. He has created dedicated servants to satisfy his will by tracing the family of Sint Lords.

"Then my father was right…"

"Your father – whom we know found the frozen alien – is in the greatest danger." Ira was glad that Shev'la found him. He had been delaying the visit to the Khan family uncertain how it would have transpired and now all was made easy by curiosity's motivation.

"My father?" asked Shev'la thinking about how Ira knew and if he did how many others may know this truth.

"Your father. His public meetings are creating a resistance to Zorath's will and he has taken notice. It is much more than the meetings really, but anyway, you must make him stop."

"Nothing can stop my father's obsessions."

"But you must. Zorath's crusaders are entering all the urbas to enforce his very will. Those that have resisted have been vanquished without cause or concern. We are fortunate that they have yet to arrive, but they will come sooner rather than later. You must stop your father. He must cease, at least temporarily, his public work. I have tried and not succeeded." What Ira failed to divulge to the cryptographer was his extended efforts to protect Tulai Khan and his ideas. Two assassins were paid off not to kill Tulai, as well as zorn sent into the underworld to keep them distracted and uninterested. It may have been the lack of execution that made the Ice King focus a little harder.

"My father will certainly not heed my words," said Shev'la.

"You must try, Khan," said Ira, adding a tone that was two notches away from pleading.

Shev'la understood its intent. "I will approach him tonight."

"Good. That is a start."

"It is the uncertainty of his stubbornness that concerns me," said Ira.

"It is a family trait," added Khan.

Chapter 3

DAYS OF research and presentations became intensified and Tulai found himself weakening at the demands of his new life's purpose. He had spent the total of his halation inventing, making things from nothing save his own cerbind. Few could achieve such things, and so, few did. It was the blessing and the curse of the inventor for they became possessed with the power of creation. He did not know that it would have put an entire planet at jeopardy nor did he foresee the loss of so many that he loved. Entans condemned to the effects of inventions, he thought. Invention was a talent and those who wielded it were superior to armies of arvicians. Creation, it seemed, was the root of all corruption and given to the wrong of cerbind was the spell of extinction.

He finished late that night after a seminar in Ceramin Square where thousands of entans came to listen to his speech on harmonizing life on Seranor. Most were young, much like his seed's age, and they were open to his ideas. Many of them did not accept the growth of mercanomics and technology believing that they polluted the planet with greed and that this greed would spell the end. The use of zorn had increased as if pushed into the hands of Seronians like candy to a seed's palms. New forms of communication mediums, such as the captivating palpazine, surfaced and proliferated new ideas capturing the attention of all, but Tulai was restricted to his own eloquent speeches. Shev'la had come late in the seminar this night and stood in the back quietly watching the quiet crowd. When he finished, many followers stayed around to ask questions but there was one very tall luto who was pacing back and forth around the crowd looking left and right as if waiting for something or preparing for something. He did not hesitate and approached the stranger.

"The seminar is finished. Time for all to leave," said Shev'la.

"I leave when I have finished," said the stranger.

Shev'la turned in combat position and withdrew his batier. "No, you leave now!"

"You are too quick in judgment, young luto." The stranger did not seem frightened by the drawn batier.

"Go or be gone."

"Put your little rod away and do not bother me further or I will be angry."

"This is my final warning," said Shev'la.

He ignored him. Shev'la jumped in to strike to injure not to kill but the stranger moved with unmatched speed leaving nothing for Shev'la to hit but his long coat.

"Stubborn fool." The more than two-meter-tall luto removed his ruined coat revealing his hardened over-sized limbs through his thin shirt. His only weapon was his body. Shev'la's batier clanged upon his arms and legs, leaving no mark or damage, as if made of polished rock. Despite acrobatics and dodging, several hits struck the seed of Tulai bruising him where they hit until he was down on the ground from the pummeling.

"My purpose exceeds my anger. You are fortunate. I shall not spare you next time," said the stranger while slowly walking away. Shev'la picked himself up then sat on one of the public seats with his head down. He knew that he had been taught some lesson just now but wasn't quite sure what it was. He wasn't turning out to be much of an opponent. The stranger had complete control over him with only his body that the batier could not match. Only the body. It felt like he was made of rock but he was an entan like me, he thought to himself, still puzzled. Another mismatched opponent. It was becoming a bad habit and he began to doubt his usefulness in combat.

Shortly after the seminar had finished, Tulai came and sat beside his seed. His face was weary, more weary than even the intense days of invention back in Ulaq.

"Are you okay, Shev'la?" asked Tulai, needing a confirmation that his seed was all right.

"Okay. I'm okay," said Shev'la, massaging his limbs.

"You look bruised."

"I was playing around and...I ended up getting hurt." He didn't have the corius to explain the stupidity of his latest action.

"Haste makes waste...We should return. I am sure that Mareenth waits on dinner for us," Tulai said while adjusting the materials he carried.

"Father?" Shev'la sat with his head down.

"Yes?"

"Are you not afraid of Zorath?" He raised his head looking directly at his father and could not tell him as direct as Ira would have wanted. No, he could say nothing more than to show concern for his father.

"I fear him less than myself and what I have to do."

"But these speeches, father, they create attention, if Zorath knew—" Shev'la grew more animated until stopped by his father's hand upon his head.

"I have learned, my dear seed," started Tulai, "that life is not a choice, it is chosen for you." He brushed his seed's hair and smiled at his accomplishment. All would not be lost. "Fear is not in doing, it is in failing to do. Seranor chose me to speak for she is far wiser than I could ever be and my only choice was to accept this as my truth, just as you will one day accept yours." Shev'la lost all his original thought. Even Ira's comment lost its value after he saw the star of wisdom in his father's eyes. Age was never wasted on the old.

"How will I know what that is?" Shev'la asked.

"It is always there and we often see it in disbelief as I have done in my life. Believe what you see and you will know."

"Can I believe what I do not see, father?"

"This is the way of belief. This is the way of Seranor."

Tulai and his seed walked home peacefully. Mareenth did not eat with them and chose to stay in her room. Shev'la decided to sleep in the kitchen to avoid confrontation. It was fortunate that he wasn't meeting Ira on the next day. He wouldn't be happy with the result of their talk.

IN THE empty streets of Casus echoed the lone footsteps of a young luto, Peel, running at full pace. He was sweating heavily now for he had been running like this for half a day; his body was caked with dirty clay with eyes fixed on his destination. He ran taking the most efficient route and sometimes found himself jumping walls or climbing over low buildings and it did not bother him.

Finally, as the morning was approaching in full he saw the bright sign of the Ice Scabbard and ran towards the front. The portal swung wide open hitting one of the locals in the arm, his scream caught the attention of the now half-filled tavern who all turned to see the dirty young luto gasping for breath.

"What the farck is your problem?" someone yelled from a nearby table.

"Yah, you morbfarck!" said another.

Peel continued to gasp and then tried to speak but could not. He collapsed on the floor breathing uncontrollably. The angry luto with the bruised arm walked over with the intention to hit him. He decided against it.

"You farck!" said the bartender, Tengal, deathly obese and loudmouthed. "You can't just walk in here and do what you want. This is a private place and anyone of these patrons can cook your ass anytime they choose." Tengal threw up his left arm, straight as straight, and Peel's helpless body flew to one of the pillars supporting the roof, held fast by Tengal's arvic casting. "You farck! I've seen many get killed for less in Casus."

Peel was winded again and struggled to speak to no avail. Tengal rotated his hand at the wrist and a sphere of cold wrapped itself around Peel. It froze his skin so that it hurt to the touch.

"You farck!" yelled Tengal. "Walk in here like that again and I'll squeeze the farcking milk out of your body!" He released the spell and lumbered away, proud of his short list of arvic intimidation spells.

Tengal Gal·net had always dreamed of becoming an arvician, even dared to dream of reaching the level of the great arvician Quazol who had battled a Nivator in the earliest of days before disappearing from the land. But his thick headedness and poor attitude regarding life in general left him with little choice; and he nabbed the zorn making opportunities that were presented when his mother died and left him a valuable estate. He sold it off and poured his wealth into the Ice Scabbard; he had preferred things of a chilly nature, his character reflected some of that.

A minute or two passed. The tavern guests were talking again. Young Peel sat up on his haunches warming his skin and then tried again to let out verse.

"It...comes..."

"Who comes?" asked the luto with the sore elbow and added the snicker of sarcasm: "Your mother, seed?" He laughed.

"No, no. Whit—white...white crusader...the crusader..."

"It approaches Casus?" the luto asked, replacing all smiles with seriousness.

The young luto nodded.

"How do you know?" he said in a sarcastic tone.

"...I saw it...it is coming..."

"When?" someone from another table asked.

"By the middle day at its pace," he said finally catching his breath. "The white crusaders approach and they come with others. Twenty-two in all. Twenty-two."

News of the white crusader coming spread throughout Casus like aqua flowing through an empty drinking straw. All Seronians became apprehensive about what would happen. They had heard the stories. It seemed that everyone was not willing to do anything until they could more clearly see the future which by now had become bleak.

Tulai had arranged for a mid-day seminar in the center and was unchanged by the news, so Shev'la had no choice in the matter and this did not make Mareenth any happier. At the house she had made it succinct in the clearest of words that he should not support his father on his own suicidal crusade and that should bad things happen she could not guarantee her support for him. Shev'la felt like the sponge, squeezed of his emotional energy by the only two remaining ceramin that he loved, and decided to be with his father for he feared that his father, from what Ira had said, was in great danger this day and that Mareenth would be okay. How wrong he was.

Chapter 4

A SCORE of riders reached the town, most wore sparkling white armor · unusual considering their long travels. At the head were two tall figures wearing full plate ceramic armor. The one on the left wore translucent blue armor with a full black helm whose face shield was translucent white. On his right hip was a white rader on a white chain girdle. The other wore a bright white suit of armor with a red helm and a black face upon it and carried a black rader on a black girdle. The other riders wore a bluish chain suit with a quaff. On their left hip was a one-handed black rader, less exceptional than that of the first two riders, and a tunic flowed over their body with a sign, on the upper left corner – a thick white strike above a large rectangular-shaped eye, the eye of Zorath: Ice Timor. A pair of matching dark blue, rectangular glasses covered their eyes lengthwise.

Groups of four dispersed themselves into the urba with two groups separately led by the leaders. The blue armored figure went to the Ice Scabbard. Many other adventurers had come to witness this monumental event, some had never tasted any adventure except in their dreams. Even young lutos and lutas were here hiding in the background and watching. The heavily armored crusader bore the symbol of a white circle on a blue background beside the strike above the eye. Before entering it stopped momentarily then went through the front portal. The four chain warriors stood outside in formation. The blue armored stranger positioned itself in the center of the tavern unafraid and unnerved. All eyes turned and mouths dropped silent.

Tengal came out from his stylistic counter muttering, "Once was enough," then removed his short apron and walked with all his excessive weight towards the crusader. The floor shook from his heaviness. "Get the farck out of my tavern!" he yelled to no reaction. He was a cocky luto since he was young; learned at young age to speak up for what he wanted, never satisfied with what he was given. He grew up bold and uncaring and chose to open the tavern so that he could demonstrate his boldness to others. He was also aware that rumors and reality never matched. As far as he was concerned this warrior or crusader of Zorath or whatever it wanted to be called was an exaggeration. A rumor without substance. A joke. "We don't welcome helmed morbfarckers in here!" The crusader did not turn to pay attention to him until he had arrived to stand directly in front of him.

"Can you understand my words?" Tengal was a large man, nearly twice the width of the crusader and nearly as tall with his high boots on. He moved closer to the helm. "Get the farck out, you morbfarck!" He looked inside and saw a space of absolutely nothing. "Probably too ugly to show his face," he said, laughing and half the tavern laughed with him. Then he defocused his eyes to see his own reflection in the helm's white face and immediately backed away grabbing his head and started crying, and as he cried, milk came out of his skin, gushing out as if his body was a balloon filled with the liquid. Half a minute of absolute horror passed, all the tavern patrons in shock, until all of his milk ran dry and an empty sack of what was once entan collapsed on the floor in a pool of its own juice. Utter fear gripped the once adventurous audience.

A lone figure, simply dressed in plain cora clothing and long, ragged and grayish hair started walking toward the front portal and, because of the positioning, had to pass the armored crusader. The mysterious luto walked by the stranger and as he passed an arm extended to stop him but the ragged luto kept walking and the gauntleted hand missed him as if it grabbed thin air. Even with his lightening reactions, by the time the crusader wanted to react the plain luto had reached the portal and walked out the building. Not bothered, the crusader turned to face the crowd. His helm shifted left to right and a perfect guess would have been that it was scanning the tavern for something or someone. Several patrons followed suit and dashed as fast as they could instead of walking. A confident adventurer-type with longish hair decided that he could walk out slowly too if the first could. But as he walked in front of the crusader, a pristine left gauntlet touched his shoulder and the luto stopped.

"Let go of me," Confidence said as an icy chill cooled his milk. But just as he finished his last word his entire right chest froze solid. Confidence died instantly. Not bothered, the crusader continued to scan then sensing some elusive resistance in the crowd he spoke: "I am Kalorian-Sint and speak for your future Ice King—King Zorath." Kalorian started in a synthetically produced voice that resonated a flat pitch without rhythm. "I seek the one known as Tulai Khan. Those who know of him will speak or cease to exist. This is my first and last demand."

Not a word was spoken. Kalorian-Sint turned his head slightly as he searched the room once more. He was sensing for someone, that someone was hidden well. Suddenly, the portal pushed open and the same tall luto that downed Shev'la on the previous night was there. He was much more prominent now, still wearing no armor but this time holding a hand-and-a-half black-blue batier in his hands. The two tall figures stood and faced each other for some time before the unarmored finally spoke.

"I am E-Non and you are not welcome here, Sint."

Kalorian ignored him and continued his scanning.

"Sint!" screamed E-Non as he prepared his batier. Kalorian raised his right hand towards him and a force of arvicity blew the unarmored luto through the portal and ripped out a three meter hole out of the front wall of the tavern sending cora and ceramic and one body outside. E-Non fell hard, surprisingly uninjured. He got up leaving the mark of his fall in the clay beneath his feet.

Kalorian traced his prey and turned his hand in its direction. A long, black haired luto revealed himself. He was cloaked and fought against the powerful spell that pulled at him from an unseen force. E-Non reappeared at the front, this time without hesitation or warning he leapt into the air raising his two-handed batier high so as to land directly on the blue armored crusader. Kalorian adjusted, withdrew a translucent, quattro-bladed rader in his left and parried the heavy-handed strike. A brilliant flash of flamma filled the entire tavern as two weapons of power clashed and tested their master's forging. Split seconds later, E-Non landed with only half his batier in hand. The other half pierced a young luta through the chest and had killed her instantly. Kalorian sheathed his undamaged rader.

Unperturbed, the broken batier was dropped and E-Non grappled the Sint crusader by the head and after moments of abnormal strength managed to remove the black helm before being pushed off meters away into the counter that left him stunned. A head of dark blue hair on blue skin with eyes of translucent white bordered with black stared at him without anger or feeling or anything that could be of entan making. It neither spoke nor moved but a shrill louder than any could bear filled the room and paralyzed everyone including E-Non. The cloaked luto was held fast on a rear pillar. A ball of flamma sprung forth from the Sint's hand and erupted into a radiated orange burst in the crowd of frightened patrons. The tavern glowed and was hazy for long moments as the five-meter diameter ball incinerated all within its bounds and burned a crater into the ground.

As Kalorian-Sint refitted his helm, all the patrons evacuated the tavern at fast pace screaming for their lives except E-Non who grappled him again. E-Non was a practitioner of the ice fist and was training to be a Nivaton, master ice warrior. The Sint's alien strength proved no match even for his own enhanced fortitude and he was thrown and beaten around until he neared the length of his mortality.

At that point, two other riders came inside to take E-Non's body with them. Kalorian walked up to the held-fast entan, looking him over to take his knowledge. The white flash of his rader cut through the pillar and the captive in one fell swoop. Pieces of the roof caved in.

The once popular tavern, emptied of all ceramin and thoroughly destroyed, was closed down.

Tengal's mother wouldn't be earning any return on her seed's investment.

A HALF-HOUR later, Tulai was standing in the center of the square preparing for his presentation. A small crowd had gathered, not as large as previous ones, and were standing instead of sitting. Shev'la was pacing back and forth worried about Mareenth and Cal'la. As much as he wanted to be with them he could not leave his father like this. His father, by now, had become distant when he spoke and was in a strange way accepting his destiny which was certain.

Tulai spoke boldly about his opinions until he winded down his speech: "Remember what has been learned. She is our planet and she is dying. If she dies, how will we live? We won't. Physical life for us is limited. I once thought that I could extend our mortality. Instead, I realized a greater truth. Greater truth? It is funny I speak this way now about greatness.

"We are already immortal from the touch of mother Seranor. As long as she lives, you and me can never stop existing. We will only change form, that is all. We will be transformed!" he said, thrusting a clenched fist into the air. "I will always live in you and it is my task in life to save our true mother and to prevent the extinction of our species. Without her we cannot exist and there are those who want this to be a reality but I tell you here and now

— we must resist at all cost or there will be no more tomorrow.

"We must remove the corruption on our planet. Cut it out like a disease before it spreads. Seranor is in danger from the Nivian who will soon become a god on planet Aquanomicus and none will be able to stop him once he has attained the levels none of us can match neither in width nor breadth nor depth. Remember your mother for she loves you still and forgives you for your mistakes."

After hearing him, Shev'la feared this the most. He lost his mother and brother and his only family was his father. For this he had to possibly sacrifice the luta he loved. He began to sweat profusely not being able to choose then at the last moment he decided to go see Mareenth. He quickly ran as his father began taking questions at the seminar without him. Nothing will happen, Shev'la thought. About half a kilometer away he heard the roar of a large crowd, the area that he had left, that put fear into his corius. He glanced once toward the direction of Mareenth trying to decide again before another loud roar called him to run as fast as he could back to the center.

He arrived in time to see a tall, fully armored warrior cast a blue-hued spell onto his father who deflected it into the nearest building disintegrating nearly half of it upon contact as well as some bystanders who were there watching. His father stood without fear or anger and faced the armored Sint crusader. The crowd that had once gathered had dispersed to a safe distance several hundred

meters away. Kalorian drew his rader to parry a
spell from Tulai's hands before flashing directly in
front of the unarmed inventor. All around them was
evidence of damage to buildings, streets and even a
handful of dead entans. No other interfered.

Shev'la wasted no time, withdrew his curved
bastion and rushed the powerful crusader knowing
only that he must try.

The inventor and the invented faced each other in
calm resolution. Tulai turned to see Shev'la and his
eyes sparkled a satisfied smile the moment before
his own nexa.

Kalorian struck twice with ease, first a deep stab
through the abdomen and then a diagonal cut from
left to right that sliced Tulai's body into two pieces,
before Tulai flashed his dying upper torso away from
the crusader. Shev'la arrived to see his father some
hundred meters to his right collapsed on the ground,
struggling to stay upright on two hands and no lower
body. Kalorian turned to face his seed. Shev'la,
yelling profusely, held his bastion with both hands
and struck more times that he could remember until
he could not strike anymore with his snapped
weapon. It had snapped twice, and though would
have killed a luto of normal stature many times
over, there was not one mark on Kalorian's armor.
The Sint laughed slow and sinister. Shev'la fell in
exhaustion and tears. "Father!" he cried out.
"Father!" Kalorian pointed the long translucent
white rader at the crying luto. The blade radiated a
flammic hue. Shev'la could feel its fiery touch on his

porcelan skin and now smelled his own imminent death.

"Your family is at end," said the crusader, dryly.

Just then a windy breeze blew the Sint's tunic open. Kalorian raised his head to sense and caught the image of a loosely dressed figure approaching him in erratic flight. He swung to strike hitting only air. The figure passed over Shev'la, picked him up without stopping and continued on its way. Several more rader slices missed and a spell came from Kalorian, it too missed the hazy figure carrying Shev'la's body, striking the crowd and killing six of them instantly. The figure disappeared around a distant building. Kalorian, not bothered, returned to his troops with his main task accomplished.

Shev'la regained his orientation enough to see a luto of ragged grayish hair, a young face without marks, and simple clothes, place him safely upon the ground.

"I am Nao," he said. "Rest here, you will be safe. They will leave soon," He then left as if a gust of wind picked him up and took him away in one fell swoop.

"Who are—" But no one was there. He got up and walked wearily to where his father lay last. He was still there. In the middle of a pool of milk sat two halves of what was once a great inventor and the last remaining direct family of Khan.

Tulai was still alive for seconds too short to count. "Shev…find it…find…"

He died.

Shev'la cried for many hours, cried for his mother, cried for his brother and cried for his father and cried for his cursed life. Soon the well of tears ran dry as did the luto's aspirations. Killing the father had also killed the kol of the seed. Maybe Kalorian-Sint had known that anyway. Mareenth came by much later and held him tight to her caring porcelan skin. But in her eyes were waiting words that would soon emerge and announce their feelings.

Chapter 5

HE RESTED that night in the street refusing to
abandon the last living memory of his father: The
place of his slaughter. The third day came, the Sint
Crusaders had left the evening before, and a funeral
was hastily put together by Tulai's best students.
That night, Shev'la returned to the bed in his cell
after his father's burial. Ira came by later in the
evening bringing a gift for him. Mareenth had
already gone out after Shev'la had fallen asleep.
Ira's face was sullen and contemplative. Shev'la
woke when Ira entered. He had many questions in
his head and he cared not for the timing or his
energy.

"What happened? Why have these crusaders come here? Why was my father killed? Did you know about this? Did you?" asked Shev'la in a weakened voice, desperate for answers to his confusion and delusion.

"They are the servants of Zorath on business for the Nivian King," replied Ira.

"What business?"

"Your father taught Zorath many things after he was discovered. He did not care then to see the consequences that would follow."

"What are you saying?—That my father caused his own death."

"The white crusaders are created from your father's now famous theories of reanimation albeit of a different form."

"My father had no intention—"

"Zorath has distorted it to suit his own purpose. He is Nivian following ora and is never concerned with the ways of opus except when it regards how he may wipe it out."

"What are these crusaders? I struck him without any effect…"

"They are the Sint Crusaders, reanimated to serve Zorath and his raking of the land."

"Reanimated—"

Ira had looked away with his eyes the entire time. It was at first glance that he caught the young entan's despairing eyes and they weakened him inside. He felt the need to explain without the force to stop it. His late father Amid would not have agreed.

"The Sint Lords were once Karul, Nivian descendants enchanted with select traits of their ancestors, of the first family of Karul that came on Seranor nearly nine thousand tios ago. Also blue skinned with hair a deeper shade of the same, these handsome beings had no emotion and only predictable reaction to situations. Their voice was cold, dark and monotone as such that of most Nivians from Nivata, and unlike Zorath whose body had absorbed much from its environment and exposure, and birthed a new form. The Sints were highly efficient, strategic, intelligent, and maintained an intense level of discipline on all areas of interest and disinterest. I know of this story well for they once nearly exterminated my entire family if not for House Draconus.

"Lord Kalorian-Sint, the father of all the Sints, harvested arvicity and learned to store it in milk and bone. He spent lengthy periods in arvic rivers to build up power over long periods. Because of his intense dedication to being the greatest Arvicerer on Seranor; he reserved his mating energy and redirected it into his art to multiply his ability to manipulate denser arvic forces; he only mated once and produced six female and six male Karuls. The twelve Sints, identical twins who were destined to die from that which created them, all studied arvicity and the ways of batier. The Sint troop became powerful Arvicerers and captains using black lutium-based weapons, all single-faced batiers in their left hands, and had great ability in manipulating arvicity. They became Crusaders and led their own ranks of cerbors and morbs, and had the most respect and fear among the other handful of Karulians. Seronians dared not defy the wills of any Sint Crusader, and those who forgot were obliterated and forever removed from the planet's surface; some were horribly scarred to remind others at the taste of defiance.

"After one thousand, two hundred and forty tios, all the Sints became sick and were dying from a rare disease where their milk repelled arvicity from the body and drained life away. Kalorian used his power, after consulting with the Seranivas, to create a series of arvic potions to counteract the process and to stabilize the mysterious disease while he searched for a permanent cure to stop his family from dying. Seronians took it as blessing from Seragorn and more of them dedicated their lives as Sagmal during that particular tio.

"Upon attacking Seronians to wipe them out, they met with Family Draconus, a family dedicated to producing the best warriors and arvicians capable of uniquely manipulating arvicity. Our House had already been severely sacked with only a few survivors left including my father's father.

"After the Sints had effectively wiped out an entire urba and were planning another attack on a city of Kozoty itself, Brulizar Draconus, father of Issachar Draconus, who was master Arvician of unique talent, went to the Sint camp and after infiltrating a toughly guarded post, broke in with eight other warriors and lured out Kalorian into the open courtyard. Once there, Brulizar cast a spell that reorganized the arvic reception and transmission in Kalorian's body so that all arvic spells would be drawn out of him and back into Seragorn. Each cast he made would only cause him to be weaker.

"Before he had chance to leave, Brulizar accepted his death for bringing down the czar of the Karulians. Brulizar's spell was the ultimate pain for Kalorian for he could no longer create the arvic potions for his family nor did he have time to find the cure to their disease. All twelve Sints became increasingly weak and then, one-by-one, dropped. They soon ceased to exist after that and were buried in a mountain. The binding of the Karuls against Seronians was finally broken and the Seronians became free once again.

"Kalorian, after failing to save his seeds and using the powers of one of the seven pieces of an ancient set—"

"The Arvinstrum..." Shev'la filled in.

"Kalorian lifted a sheet out of Seranor's thick hide and buried them all in ritualistic fashion sealing the tomb so that all who tempted to open it would get drained of their arvic energy as was done to him. He would curse those who tried to disturb what was taken away from him. Quarka, a female Malkar, was then summoned to kill Kalorian who could no longer accept his pain and whose anger prevented him from destroying himself. She buried him in a lake now called Lake Kalorian by the River of Sints. Quarka did so, chose to remain on Seranor, and became a powerful adversary to the Serag."

"So the Sints have come back. They have been reanimated as servants to Zorath," said Shev'la.

"Kalorian-Sint was the first to be reanimated by Zorath but not before he constructed the *Qari*, a set of powerful ancient arvicity and elemental power devices that we have yet to fully understand. It has taken Zorath 30 tios to recover after raising Kalorian-Sint and constructing the first Qari, but now he has found a new energy source to accelerate the process.

"Kalorian then went out to raise his family to once more reign terror on the land. Once all thirteen Sint bodies had been retrieved, Zorath preserved them and began construction of a Qari for each so that they may represent all his desires upon planet Seranor. So that all Seronians can share his pain and serve for his final purpose – occupation of Nivata and the annihilation of Rascoth, the great Nivian King."

"Then he is unstoppable..."

"Do not be so certain of that."

"I am certain of one thing – death. The death of my family. The eventual death of Shev'la Khan."

"You must rest, Shev'la. I have overstayed my visit and must go."

"Answer me one thing, Ira."

"If I—"

"Are you afraid of Zorath?"

Ira turned to face the exit. Walked to the archway rotating his head at a slight angle to his back and gave a short dip with his chin. "Now." He walked out silent as ever.

Shev'la whispered. "And so am I." He fell softly asleep to be comforted by his dreams.

EMPTY STREETS suited the hollow insides of the beautiful luta walking along them. Mareenth walked slowly, almost cautiously. She was remembering a time when life had grown peaceful, fertile and happy. A happiness she had since lost in Casus. She never told her husband of her past as a prostitute thinking that it was not important in their relationship and that she was no longer that person. But her pain for living here for the past 50 tios had burned her inside and now with Tulai murdered she no longer felt that she nor Shev'la would need to stay. He was lucky to have survived and they could have a normal life together and only hoped that Zorath's power would weaken over time by others who would take over Tulai's revolution. Something deep inside of her did not fully believe this dream. She knew of his love but also felt the need of living with her husband. Since the time of Calil's death, Shev'la had adopted many of his father's habits: dedication to research, development of the self, and construction of new communications devices. "Inventors" they were called.

Mareenth walked and walked until she found herself in the area she once called home. It had been layered over with a gloss of a red ceramic surface that left a smooth and pure look about it and ignited the senses beyond just sensuality and into existentiality. She entered the semi-familiar building from her past and asked the first entan she met about some of her friends.

"I search for some friends," Mareenth said.

"We all search for friends," answered a mature luta attending the front entrance.

"No, they work here. Do you know a Tey?"

"Maybe."

"It's important. Tey, Gel and Saq, do you know where they are now?" The attendant looked at Mareenth, staring at her features, then noticing something familiar.

"You're Mar, aren't you?"

"Was," replied Mareenth.

"I heard of you. You don't remember many of those who come and go but I've heard mention of your name."

"Listen, have you seen these lutas?"

"Tey and Saq are dead. They drank too much anaprimo while have excessive sex. This shat is everywhere now. I've never seen so much of the elemental juice."

"Dead—And Gel, where is Gel?"

"She gave birth to a seed and moved to the other building across the street."

"Do you know exactly where?"

"No. Just ask the old luta downstairs wearing the triangular glasses. She'll know." The attendant pointed to an area across the way.

Mareenth heard loud thundering footsteps from atop the stairs, she immediately recalled Jod, the Malkar who killed her friend, and it froze her in her tracks. Time slowed. Her corius was running fast and the footsteps came closer. She again experienced the horror from so many years ago.

"Luta, are you feeling okay?" the attendant asked.

The footsteps came closer. The luta behind the counter reached out her hand and twisted Mareenth's head from its fixed position. It snapped her out of her current state and put her staring at an extremely large luto with the face of a rough clay mountain side and eyes covered with black triangular glasses. When she realized that it wasn't a Malkar, she felt as if her life had been saved. The luto walked slowly wearing mismatched plate and chain armor, his limbs bulged from every direction as he carried a heavy two-handed clavus in one hand, and she could only imagine his massive strength. He threw down a key card as he walked by hitting Mareenth with his shoulder without even noticing that he did. She was knocked back into the wall.

"Va!" he said in a morb's voice and walked out.

"Come back soon," replied the attendant.

Mareenth, calm that she wasn't in any danger, looked at the card that he had dropped down. It read "51".

"Is he a regular?"

"Griz?"

"Is that his name?"

"Yeah, he comes here all the time when he's in town and he always takes number 51."

"Some things don't change," said Mareenth, regarding the attraction of some lutos to keep the same prostitute. "Thank you for your help."

"Right-O, Mar."

By morning, the usual sounds of Casus have been replaced by a serenity and suspension of belief. Many more than usual were on the street still wasted from ingesting too much anaprimo mixes. The morning was delayed as if everything was uncertain that it would still be here. Mareenth neared her building, thinking about Shev'la and her life, and after an entire night without sleep was without any resolution to her dilemma. A luto tossed a rounded palpazine to her and she briefly viewed the major news of the day about the damage done to Casus this week. The Institute of Arvicians was completely sacked and an area of two or three hundred meters around it was demolished from a war of arvicity. The Ice Scabbard was closed down for repairs for one to two weeks and three high level Captains of the Seronian Guard were assassinated with a Captain T. Rain as one replacement, as well as other news; as she caught the smaller stories she saw an all too familiar name and quickly ran inside to tell Shev'la. She burst into his room but he was not there; instead he was lying on the floor belly down.

"Shev, get up. Look at the palpazine!"

"Mareenth?" He said with his head still down. "What happened to you? I worried the entire night."

"I'm all right," she replied. "Take a look at this!"

He grabbed the translucent cora sphere, palpazine, that had become a mainstay of modern society. He called the word and the article appeared in the air in front of him.

"What—"

She read it out loud for him, "Ira Levin, leader of an underground resistance, had disappeared after his operations were sacked late in the night."

"Where did he go?"

"It doesn't say."

"Ira cannot disappear, not unless he chooses to. This palpazine lies. It is that simple."

"But Shev, what about your job?"

"That is also gone if Ira and his business is dead. Death fills my life once again."

"What's going to happen to us, Shev?"

"I don't have an answer right now, Mareenth. I don't have any answers. We must be strong together."

"What of Cal'la?"

"She is fine...we will be fine," he said without the normal optimistic certainty that always resonated in his voice.

"I don't want to be fine. I want to be happy," she said.

"Are you not happy with me?" he asked.

"Yes, but you've changed, Shev. I know that the deaths have affected you, more than you care to realize, but I am not happy anymore."

"We have survived the extinction of a town—we have been free for the past 49 tios and now you tell me that you are not happy. I thought at the beginning that you would readjust and maybe you would learn to fit into the urba. What is it with you, Mareenth?"

"I did not tell you before because I thought that you didn't need to know but now I feel that you must know about my past. I used to live in Casus."

"That I know."

"I lived here as a prostitute."

"That I didn't know—A prostitute?"

"Yes, for sixty tios. I have enjoyed more sex than most lutas can dream about. I was young and didn't realize it so clearly as now but I do not regret my past, so to put me here again I feel that I have not grown as I should have and have; instead, been put into the bowel of my own seedhood.

"Can you not see, Shev? You escaped your town but I have returned to mine. We are at ends like this and I can no longer continue. It drives me to scratch the walls and to bite the ceramic table in our room. I grow more miserable by the day."

"I cannot give you what I myself do not have," said Shev'la.

"But you can learn to feel it. To understand what I need," said Mareenth.

"It has been my whole life, all my days since I can remember that love has not touched deep in me. I cannot tell you what it looks like, only to know that what you ask now I cannot give."

"Do you not understand my need at least?"

"Yes, I think so."

"Then where is the problem?"

"Your need is not mine; my need is not yours."

"Shev, don't do this to me, to us."

"I'm not trying to do anything. I don't want to make you believe that I am something that I am not. It's not fair to hold back one who can love because of one who cannot," he said.

"I can help you," she said. "I want to help you. Come with me and leave this place."

"Help is beyond where I have reached now."

"Why are you doing this? Why?"

"I cannot continue to hurt you."

"You're afraid of hurting yourself."

"You should go and find your needs. I need to stay."

"You selfish bastard!" she cried out. "You're just protecting your own insecurity."

"I do not know why or how long, only that I need to stay."

"What will you do here?"

"I will live out the rest of my short life."

"You can live! You can. But you are afraid to fight what you cannot see."

"I don't want to fight anymore."

"You and your theories are just an empty bridge."

"My father had the theories. I am only the seed of a murdered parent. It does not matter anymore."

"Go to your life!" she yelled and was standing now. "Go! Because I don't want to be with you."

"Nothing matters to my cursed life," he said.

"I hate you! I hate you! Selfish morb!" Mareenth walked up to get Cal'la before arriving at the portal to the outside. "Go play with the wind. You hear me. Go because that's all you're worth Shev'la

Khan...the great Khan who brings back kols—has none himself. Go!"

Mareenth and Cal'la left Casus that same morning. Her leaving ripped out a part of himself and he was helpless to change it.

From this point, Shev'la would degrade into a flicker of his former self and when he shut the portal to his cell on that very day he had no intention of re-opening it.

Chapter 6

LIFE AND death. Two interactive devices to keep the struggle rich and rewarding. It could be said that survival is the struggle for life, a destiny built into the design of it all, and that death was the result of an exhausted life, without vigor to continue forward. Life was the brightness while death, the stillness and ending of all things.

What if, thought Shev'la, death was the bright flamma and that in death life reached its climactic point, then instead of building a purpose to live we should build a purpose to die.

We all exist on the fuse of death and whereas many believed that death was the sputter of that luminous fuse, it became clearer to the seed of Khan that, in fact, the fuse's burning brought entans closer to illumination, and in those last moments of life an entan's total existence became amplified. Death was the brightness. But surely one cannot become bright in their waiting. We must move into it. I must live for death and at the last tip of my fuse shall I demonstrate all the stored potential of my existence. Strive for death using life as the fuse and brightness will be the richest.

Weeks later after not leaving his room for that long, Shev'la took his clothes and the stack of his father's four remaining manuscripts aptly titled "Reanima 1 through 4" in a backpack and stepped out the front portal. The spattering of clay he had survived on were enough only to keep his existence intact. Nothing more. He was without direction or plan only knowing that he must move or he would cease to move, permanently. To burn the fuse became his determination.

He marched excitedly, rushed to arrive somewhere, rushed to leave his old self behind. Walking would not be enough for that.

On his hasty way he decided to make a stop at the Ice Scabbard for a swift drink of anaprimo with the last of his zorn. Shev'la was not one to imbibe on the juice heavily but neither were all things as before. Moments had elapsed and life had changed. Father had left him as the last remnant of the Khan family and the luta he most loved abandoned him as a scent leaves a dead body. The art of leaving was forming his trademark talent. Soon, if he continued, they would call him "The Departed". It wouldn't have been so bad. At least he would die as an embedded memory. Where would he go with no one left for him to love or be loved?

The Ice Scabbard, packed as usual inside, was surrounded by the talkative and the taxing. Outside, small-time numularians, merchants of the liberal economy, were selling their fill of oddities and strangeness to passersby. One of them caught Shev'la's attention more than it should have. It was an odd map seller wearing a pointed hat. He was too small for his yellow cora jacket but held a welcoming face. Maps, Shev'la thought, were the driving forces that begged him to escape the comforts of Ulaq and to drink the succulent fluids that life held within its matter. His seedhood thirst. More than anything, the idea brought a perked interest to his cheeks.

After all, maps were used to help those who were trying to find something and, more than any time in his life, Shev'la Khan was wanting to find a peculiar thing. He searched for an answer to his repetitive question: Why me? Obviously, no answer was returned and only confirmed to his cerbind that not all lives were filled of the same material as others. His existence became a desperate need to survive, from hour to hour. Days felt like tios and his weeks of staying at the residence felt more like 70 tios of imprisonment in the defecation of his cerbus.

"Maps, all kinds of maps to secret treasures and ancient armor. Who wants maps?" said the salestan, cheery in every verse with a piercing line of shiny gums.

Shev'la walked by.

"Entan, maybe you want a map," said the sly salestan to Shev'la. "Seek fortune and a map shall find it for you. Seek power and the map will be your guide. Seek redemption and the map is your healer. Come, take a look at my maps. We have a map for all things."

Shev'la stopped, watching the entan. "I don't need a map," he said. The salestan jerked his hip to one side in a strange fashion every time he took a couple of steps.

"We all need a map sometimes," the salestan continued quickly so that he would lose his target's interest. "When things are lost and we can no longer see the path, a map can make everything clear." Shev'la reconsidered his proposition. The appeal of finding something entered his head. It had been a long time since anything was imagined.

"What kind of maps do you have?" asked Shev'la, hesitantly. The question pulled itself out of his mouth.

"All kinds. Sit a moment and I will get all that you need." The old looking luto pulled out many maps from his large sack. Shev'la sat on the stool below and placed his backpack to his side for comfort. Map after map was thrown at him with more paragraphs than he could digest until finally a map of interest came: The map of the Arvinstrum.

"I'll take this one," said the lonely luto.

"Ah, my best map. Your eyes are good at finding bargains my youthful entan. Yes, yes. The map to the hidden Arvinstrum. Ssshhh, we must be careful when exposing such words of power near the tavern of adventure." Shev'la did not see the cracks in the salestan's deceitful mask. But that rhythmic jerking motion made him smile.

Shev'la was fully taken by him. "Yes, we must be quiet. How much?"

"It is my best and will grant whoever finds the piece s great power. Yes, great power in their hands shall be at their disposal. Are you sure that is the map you want?" The salestan went on. "The tale of the Arvinstrum is connected to Seranor herself just as anaprimo is taken in a goblet. You know, there are many qualities to anaprimo, each with their own power. Devices of old are like this. They were made using great arvic energy and this map will show you to the greatest devices ever created if you are ready for such a thing but such knowledge cannot come cheaply. No, not all of life's treasures are free."

"How much for such a map?" asked the remaining Khan.

"Five thousand zorn."

"But I do not have such wealth."

"Well, I always like to see if I can help those who search for things. My business is built on keeping finder and unfound together," the luto said then paused briefly before moving on. "You know, zorn is only one form of exchange. I could consider another form perhaps. Do you have anything of value that I might consider?"

"No."

"Say, what is it you have in your pack?'

"Nothing of real value."

"Let us look. Valueless to you may have value to me. Maybe I can trade you something for this map of superiority and control. Those who hold the Arvinstrum will rule the planet, I have heard such words. Yes. Open your pack and let us see."

Shev'la opened the backpack and revealed some clothes and the manuscripts. "Only these manuscripts are worth something of value."

"Let me see." The old luto took one and examined it closely then put it down with a saddened face. "It seems that you are right. These are of not much value."

"Would they be enough to pay for the map, sir?"

"I'm not sure. I want to help you out but I must continue my business or they will take my license away. These are difficult days. The laws change at the change of cerbind. I want to help you but I must consider."

"Please, let us make an exchange," said Shev'la, his eyes had brightened at the prospects contained on the map of the Arvinstrum. "You can have all four manuscripts for this one map. Four for one. I have no need for such things anymore and you can probably make some zorn from it."

"It *is* the map of power. Maybe the manuscripts have value – if I take them all – is that right?" asked the salestan for confirmation.

"Yes, yes."

"Do you really want the map?"

"Yes."

"And no other will know about this? If they do I will be raided by dealmakers."

"I will tell no one," said Shev'la.

"If you do not make mention of this to any others then…this one time I will agree. It is only because I feel generous and I see an entan who will be happy with his new gift."

"Thank you." Shev'la exchanged his father's manuscripts for the one map to the Arvinstrum.

Twenty minutes later, while inside the Ice Scabbard, after intently looking at the map for several minutes he noticed that the map began to fade in the flamma lighting until its definition and detail were no longer visible and was no longer there. An empty sheet of palp rested between his hands. He sat there trying to understand it at first then awoke to what had happened.

"Shat! That thief ripped me off!" Panic opened the window. My father's manuscripts? he thought, and then it hit him, the map trader, that little miserable shat, sold him a false map.

He raced outside to find an empty alcove, not even the marking of someone who had been there remained. In every direction it was plain as plain could be. Whatever happened it had long since finished, he said to himself.

He went inside to order a drink and when he went to pay couldn't find his zorn disc. "You morbfarcking, thief!" he yelled in the tavern. Luckily the new owner and bartender, Huasco, was trying to get a new crowd to come and in the generous moments of a soft opening let Shev'la go without closing the bill.

Shev'la returned to the outside, numbed and dismounted. He wandered this way and that until his feet could wander no more and he sat. He didn't notice the dirty floor or the masses of ceramin or the wind blowing his long hair. Without food, zorn, or equipment he began to relax and to accept that everything was gone. Even his wife and his only seed. Peace found its way in and he relished in it. Soaked in its tenderness and love. Finally, in the absence of anything real, he had found the fundamental caring by the eyes and altered by the touch. It was peace that became his friend. Serenity had made him drunk. After two days of peaceful living in an unmarked alcove further into the urba, the sparkle came back to his old self and he returned to the Ice Scabbard. If I have nothing, he thought to himself, then I can lose nothing. I can start anew. Live for death until the fuse becomes the flamma.

THE TAVERN was full this noon time and Huasco put him sitting with another small make-shift table. Huasco was over two meters tall, mostly coming from his long neck, and had average looks. A noticeable imperfection was positioned directly on his nose.

The noise level shook the pillars. Beside Shev'la sat a hulking luto wearing roughshod armor, a face of extreme brutality, and wore black triangular glasses on his face. The entan hulk had just rearranged another's face making it a permanent part of the flooring after the unknown luto touched his armor. The message was clear. He didn't like it when others touched him. Shev'la had arrived just as the body was being dragged on its way out. It left a line of white milk which the attendants quickly mopped up.

It was fortunate that the young Khan arrived after the incident. In his current state of cerbind he might not have cared anyway. His caring for things had floated away as a kol does after death.

"I'm Shev'la. How are you?" said the high spirited loner as he sat down across from the hulk.

No response.

"I'm Shev'la! How are you?!" Shev'la repeated, shouting this time.

"Sile!" the unnamed guest roared.

"I don't understand. What did you say?"

"Sile!"

"What?"

The ugly guest grabbed Shev'la whole handedly by the head and picked him off of the ground as he himself stood up.

"Sile!"

"You know I wish you would speak something I could understand," said Shev'la trying to work his mouth so that the verse was clear. "I don't want any problems, I'm just being friendly. If you don't want to talk then don't. Put me down if you will." He had no intention of fighting. It was the time of peace in his life, peace for all things but perhaps not as idealistic as he thought.

He was gently let down though his head still felt
dizzy from the lutium grasp of the over-sized entan.
The stranger sat down again and after a brief
minute of standing, Shev'la decided to sit with him,
again.

"Back you," said the entan hulk.

"Yes, I'm back. You don't know how to speak, is
that it?"

"Speak."

"What is your name?"

"I, Griz."

"I, Shev'la Khan...Shev'la."

"Khan."

"No, Shev'la Khan."

"Khan."

"Okay, Khan. You, Griz."

"I, Griz."

"Do you have a last name, Griz, or is this the
whole name?"

"Griz."

"Great. Griz Griz."

"How are things..." The two oddballs sat together
not speaking very much but telling stories with their
arms, hands and expressions. Hours passed and
soon the tavern was empty except for only a couple
of others. Griz had come from a distant region and,
from what Shev'la could understand, his father was
a potion maker. He had lived in and out of Casus for
eighty tios and now was a member of Tri, the Cult of
Glass. Khan had read about it in the palpazine.

Tri believed that transparent ceramic glasses
could release the true power hidden in the self.

Novices first started with dark round glasses, then clear ones, then they would reach stage three which were dark and triangular in shape. The final stage were clear triangular glasses that reflected the true self. The unconfident, illiterate and ugly-faced hulk was of Karul and was chosen to do the dirty tasks in Tri. He was immensely strong and loved to fight, loved to kill and so was used for this purpose. Only by a strange occurrence did he come to the tavern. The leader of the cult, Uti-mal, had been killed two nights ago. He was reputed to be the only one on Seranor who could transform ceramic into pure glass. Griz no longer had a master and felt lost in the anger of abandonment. It was not the first time.

After a lengthy and awkward discussion, Shev'la could no longer contain himself. "You do not need a master, Griz. Who knows if the glasses ever really did anything to help you. I would guess that he had much wealth which you helped him to achieve. He needed you more than you needed him. Here, take off your glasses—"

As Shev'la touched the rims, Griz grabbed his arm and nearly snapped it at the wrist if he hadn't moved.

"Hey, hey, hey...okay...relax! Relax! I'm just trying to help...these glasses do nothing for you," Shev'la used excessive arm gestures to make certain of what he said. "You don't need them!"

"Want them."

"Yes, I know but d-o-n-t n-e-e-d them. Understand?"

"Want them."

"Okay, have them but don't say that I didn't warn you. Look inside," he said and pointed to Griz's chest. "Look inside and you will see your self. Look inside without the glasses and you will know that I am right."

"Want them."

"Yes, I heard already. Griz, I am going now but remember my words. Take care of yourself and the bill." He got up, put his left hand on Griz's shoulder and left the tavern. Griz turned to see him exit the portal then turned back facing as he was.

SHEV'LA FOUND a spot on a busy street and decided just to watch entans walking around. He had no zorn and not much else to speak of so he just sat and watched. Watching entans walk and move provided an interesting form of entertainment for more than two hours. One particular luto moved amazingly similar to someone he knew, but wasn't sure where he knew him. The hips would jerk awkwardly after each group of steps. Then he placed it, it was salestan. The old map seller except he didn't look as old as before. Suddenly he was reminded of his father's manuscripts and how important they were to him. They were his entire family now.

The map seller darted off to the right as soon as he heard Shev'la's footsteps behind him. He didn't care whose feet were following but any feet that were following him meant trouble so he ran as fast as he could. The speed and ease at which he ran proved difficult for even Shev'la's quick agility. The map seller had no real advantage, he was an expert at running while Shev'la was an expert at chasing. Round and round, high and low, turning this way and jumping that way the two continued at full charge until at last in a final breath, Shev'la jumped up and flipped over his opponent and missing his timing slightly landed directly on him, instead of in front of him, as he had intended.

Right there where they finished, Shev'la removed his dirty sash and tied the map seller tighter than a drum after knocking a drawn short batier away. He was still short of breath when he kicked the map seller a few times before turning to questions as an improved form of communication.

"Where are my manuscripts?" Shev'la asked.

"Manuscripts? What manuscripts?" said the amnesic thief.

"You know you little shat. What's your name?"

"Comifer."

"Morbshat!—What's your name?" He grabbed him by the hand and squeezed hard with both of his hands.

"Not the hand, not the hand...Boon, my name is Boon...now let go of my hand..."

"That's better."

"What do you want?"

"You remember me, don't you?"

"No. Remind me. I meet lots of different ceramin everyday."

"You stole my pack and sold me a false map."

"What are you talking about? I have never met you—" Three swift kicks in the abdomen helped him to refresh his memory. "Okay. Okay. So I sold you a bad map. There's lots of bad stuff out there."

"So Boon, you sell maps for a living?"

"Not really."

"What do you do?"

"Whatever is needed."

"You're some kind of thief, then?"

"Not a thief."

"Then what?" asked Khan.

"I exchange one for another according to what people need. I facilitate valuable exchanges and earn my living by it. I'm a marketer of sorts. It's a new profession."

"You're a thief and you stole something valuable to me and I want it back."

"You mean your pack?

"No. I mean my manuscripts." Two kicks followed.

"Oh yes, the manuscripts?" said Boon.

"Where are they? Tell me or I will break both your hands before I take you to the Seronian Guard."

"I'd be a little careful of the guard, yes, yes, there are some strange things going on—all over."

"What strange things?"

"Ever since those crusaders came to visit things have been happening, yes, yes."

"What things? Stop talking in gibberish."

"Things, things. There were several assassinations. Bet you didn't know about that. And I know one of them was, Zorn."

"The monetary system?"

"No, Zorn the invisible assassin. He is the most famous—" he stopped short looking left and right.

"Who was assassinated?"

"Captains of the Guard, an inventor, and the leader of Tri—"

"An inventor, which inventor?"

"Khan, I think, yes, yes, one called, Khan."

"Who killed him?" asked Khan, intrigued. "Murdered by the command of the Ice King, it is said."

"You are talking nonsense…in fact, we were just talking about my manuscripts until you little shat, distracted me. Where are they?"

Boon shut up, but couldn't stop from talking once Khan twisted the sash tighter on his hands.

"I don't have them," he blurted out.

"I am tiring of this," said Khan. "Where are they?"

"I sold them. Someone wanted them and I sold them. Nothing personal—"

"It is personal, you shat! You morbshat! I want them back."

"I can get them. If you pay me."

"You also stole my zorn."

"No zorn? That is a problem."

"Then you will lose both hands for your error," said Khan.

"Okay, okay, I'll get it for you but just give me some time. I need some time. If you need some zorn go see the luta with the long hair."

"Where is she?"

"She is two streets over. She's got long hair. Her name is Calwin. Tell her that Boon sent you and that she should give you as much zorn as you need. She won't give you more than Z1000 but it will cover you for several days. By then I will have the manuscripts and your pack. Okay?"

"Take me to this luta." Boon, tied at the hands, led Shev'la just as he had said two streets down to find a luta of long hair. There she was. The luta went inside and Boon stopped.

"I'll wait here," the thief said.

"No, you're coming with me," said Khan, tugging at him.

"I can't. If she sees me then she won't give you the zorn."

"Why?"

"She's very peculiar, she only talks to one entan at any one time. You see, when she was still a seed she was stricken with an illness that caused her to lose her sight when talking to two or more entans. It was the strangest thing that I heard when I heard it also, but it's true. She will become blind and mute if she sees the two of us together and then there is no way to talk to her. It has always been like this and makes it safe for me to give her zorn for when others come looking for it she cannot speak nor see them. This system has protected me from many a battle, let me tell you. I remember one battle where I..."

"All right, all right. Shut up for one minute, will you. I'll go alone. You wait here."

"No problem. I'll just stick around for a while."

Shev'la tied Boon to a post and went inside the building to find the luta. Once he saw her, he called out her name, "Calwin!" The luta turned, looked confused and turned away. Shev'la ran up and the luta started to run away. He grabbed her.

"Help!" she screamed.

"It's okay, Boon sent me."

"Who are you?"

"I'm Shev'la. Boon, your friend sent me."

"Who's Boon?"

"Boon, the skinny luto who always works with you."

"Sorry. Shev'la is it? But I don't know any Boon. Now, let go of my arm!" She was weaving a spell. He let go, slightly bewildered. "You'd better leave before I hit you or the guards come." Arvicity ran through her fingers.

"That little morbshat!" he yelled, then raced out the portal only to find what he just knew. The thief had lied to him again. That story was too much morbshat to be true. "One step further into idiocy, Shev. And you're running out of steps," he said to himself. He sat down where he lay then collapsed. He had forgotten to eat regularly over the past several days and his body finally ran out of energy. Black circles, deep and dark, revealed themselves around his eyes. They had been there some time.

A dream had filled him and in it he was walking on a thin piece of ice toward the voice of his father then he crashed through and tried to pull himself out of the hole. His body began to freeze when, from the fog, came blue-skinned Zorath speaking in the voice of his father, then he could no longer sustain himself and he fell under. It was then that he awoke and found the luta pouring cold aqua over his body. It was Calwin. Her comfortable touch and smooth skin reminded him of the wife he lost. She sang softly filling the room with love and occasionally her smooth hair would flutter over his skin just enough to remind him the pain of the love he lost.

"You...how did I...?" he asked in a weak voice.

"You fell. You have not eaten for days," she replied. "Rest." The weakness once again pulled him into a sleep. By the second time he woke there was no one around. Some of his energy had returned so he got up. He left quietly. The Departed struck again.

Chapter 7

IF THERE was a fifth perfection in entans then the wind masters could be said to possess it. Physical weapons were ineffectual on them once they had achieved the level of Wind Equist, the nameless insane master of the wind form. Equists moved directionless yet arrived at their destination. Violence, to them, was the word of the dying. In their ways to mastery they succeeded without succeeding over an opponent, fights were fought without pain, scars were never made, flesh never pierced or broken, and the land not burned; the only damage done was to their cerbinds. It became unstable, shifting as a blinding storm inside their head that granted them access to Nata's own flowing strengths.

To Shev'la, the nine Equists walking in the street as he left Calwin's residence were nine badly dressed, drunken with primo, and a month late for a hair appointment, lutos who suited the mountain lifestyle much more than the clean streets of Casus. Most of the Wind Equists had died of split cerbi; the highest masters were said to have just disappeared. But that day, Shev'la Khan did not have one millimeter of concern for the wanderers. In fact, he even began to consider the option of wandering the land as the luto without a name, as a luto unlike he was at this time. Was it possible, he considered, that I am really someone else disguised as who I am? All ideas of possibility professed themselves to his desperation. All ideas save the one he was about to meet. Finally, an end to his futility and an unexpected initiation would soon be presented to the seedling of Tulai Khan.

He headed in the direction of the raggedly dressed group, walking without formation in movements out of sync. Each step they took was simply a step forward yet contained no set pattern or rhythm. Eight of them passed the exhausted luto without acknowledgement. Khan only felt their presence as one would a soft breeze on a quiet night by a pond. One stopped shortly after. The others continued as they were.

It was the one who had pulled him to safety when his father was killed. Shev'la was sure of it. Nao had long gray hair, unkempt but clean, with a red, unmarked headband. The clothes were clearly worn and of an old style that used a basic design and the limited use of color, much fewer than in fashion now. But they were also clean. And no weapons could be seen on him even as he moved closer. Shev'la stood firmly, curious to know and not to do.

"You have lived and yet I see that you are near death again," the stranger said.

"Maybe I was to die that day and now await my death," answered Khan.

"Life and death are one in the same. Some choose one while they are in the other. It is a strange circumstance to see so many living," Nao said.

"Why did you save me?" asked Khan.

"Your father did influence the world. I could not save him," Nao said, glancing over his shoulder to his friends who had already phased out of sight.

"And now I live each day without family or love or anything that was once important to me before. It would have been better to have died. It would be the same."

"Not the same. You have what you have because you have chosen it, not because it was taken from you."

"I am nothing now without them."

"You need nothing to be—I am Nao Li-Grum. I will leave tomorrow for a long journey. As you have nothing to do, you can accompany me and my friends."

"I must find something that was lost first."

"What is that, my young friend?"

"From my father. I must find it. It is the only thing of my family that is left."

"Forget the past—find what is in front of you. It is a safer bet. In the meantime, you shall need zorn so take this, I have plenty for my simple needs, take this credit tard and use it as you will."

"I am already indebted to you for my life—"

"Indeed it is I that am indebted to you. I will feel better knowing that at least you have enough zorn to provide the basic necessities you need to live." Nao threw the tard up high so that Shev'la could catch it easily, and he did. He held it in his hand and considered the bargain.

No sense arguing. It just drains energy, he thought, before he said, "Thank you."

"Shall we enjoy a drink before I go. I, at least, am thirsty and would like to hear more about you," said Nao.

"I know of a place," said Khan, straight from reaction and not cognition.

They arrived at a small drinking tavern called Helm. Some local patrons were there quietly drinking.

"I was thinking that we would again arrive at the Ice Scabbard," said Nao.

"Too many bad things as of late at that place."

"Bad to some, but adventurers from across the land are flocking to it. It seems that death attracts the new society. Technology and danger. There will be more of that, I am sure."

"Why are you here, Nao Li-Grum? And why do you have a name? Wind followers never keep a name."

"That is true and also a long story."

"We have some time. I have nothing else but time to organize and keep me company."

"Then I suppose...it's okay. Are you sure you want to hear it?"

Shev'la nodded his head.

"My friends and I are from the Formless Fist, the original group of wind followers. We are the last."

"What happened to the others?"

"They have been separated."

"Separated?"

"Separated. Their cerbind and body had disassociated for a long period and they died in the wind."

"They all died?"

"One had in fact rematerialized in entan form..."

"What happened to him after?"

"He died...You see, Khan, when the cerbus is caressed by Nata for such a period of time there is nothing left. The original organic matter, porcelan and its pieces, had been reformulated into air, essentially. When he came out of form, his cerbus, the cerbind which made him entan was still unformed and unstable. He was not able to return its shape and in his trying, it is my guess, he missed a critical factor. It wouldn't take much to do so. The cerbind is the most delicate device ever shaped by nature and yet the most gifted. You can now understand why it hides itself behind that ceramic plate you call your skull. To see its ability would be to lose its value. All of society would surely rape it, merely for their pleasure, merely for..."

"If the cerbus is so gifted then why so few of you follow its discipline?"

"Why does one luta wear green and not red? Why does one luto carry a batier while another uses a clavus? The world is full of all things to pleasure our fantasies."

"I still do not understand something..."

"Only one thing?"

"You said your name was Nao Li-Grum, right?"

"And you want to know why I have a name and others do not?" Khan nodded in agreement. "Some of us, very few in truth, have chosen to keep our birth names. It reminds us of what we once were. That we were once with the others. That we were once fulfilling a need. It's funny to even think about it this way..."

"Why is that?"

"Names. Names shouldn't be given to you. They should be made. Once made all will know your name for it is like the sound of the wind that follows you around every corner and up every hill. Discover that wind and discover your identity."

"You mean who I am?"

"Exactly. Once known, your ability, success and more is multiplied in unknown multiples."

"If we do not need a name then why does all of society have one?"

"Names are only ways to measure and count us as is the capacity of technology. Nature is the highest form of technology ever created. Free and everlasting. Nata exists in her. She is the breath and life."

"Life. Life is empty without love." Mareenth holding Cal'la appeared in his cerbind. "Are you not lonely?" asked Shev'la.

"I have long surpassed that need, Khan. Love exists without anything."

"Maybe, but I think I need love. I miss it so. Love is like a curse that I can never touch."

"Do not try to touch it, Khan." Nao started this time more vibrant than his relaxed self, waving his arms to and fro. "Try to feel it instead. It is carried in the air. Nata brings it to all places. When you breathe, love is inside you, flowing through you, feeding your needs. When you walk, it brushes your white porcelan face and massages it's perfection. The wind brings all that you need. She shows you that there are no needs because all has already been satisfied."

"If it could be so simple—"

"It is," Nao said as a gulp of air found its way into Shev'la's nose and down inside of his chest. The air refreshed him. It gave him stability. The air washed away the bad thoughts that had been creating crevices in his head. He wanted to know more. "What is the benefit of learning the wind?"

"The wind, Khan, is Nata. She is the spirit of motion and change. She forms the basis of everything around you and inside you. It is the wind who is the unseen hero of this planet. And if you can dance with her then she will grant you abilities that enhance all that you do."

"Tell me more."

"Still impatient, I see. You must learn to dance with her. There is opportunity still. We are passing through on our way to Canyon d'Altu for the final joining with Nata."

"You will join her?"

"Yes."

"And then?"

"And then we will take our place in the protection of the planet. She needs us now more than ever."

"Is it difficult to learn the wind?"

"The challenge is not in the study but in the sacrifice. That is what many find difficult and why there are so few of us now. It is funny that entans flock to technology and, at the same time, fear the nature of the elements."

"You defeated the Sint. Was that the wind form?"

"Yes, but I did not defeat him. I merely avoided him and he did not pursue for his other business preceded me. This time we were both fortunate."

"Could you beat him?" Khan questioned him.

Nao expected this sooner and was content that Khan did live up to some of the stories about his father. The young luto was anxious but not without a shield of intelligence. "I could say either yes or no but I will just say this: Nata is the free flowing spirit in the land and the greater the force against her, the greater her power; she is unlimited because she is unencumbered. All other systems such as weapons and technology are encumbered by structure. The wind is not and will never be."

"How do you train for the wind?"

"There are many techniques, some require being in the wind, the canyons are the best places. Come with me now and you can see how we practice."

"Now?"

"Yes, are you free?"

"Well—"

"Do you want to see how we train? Now is your chance. Few will see this opportunity. We will leave tomorrow."

It was nothing more than the feeling of being wanted once again that permeated Khan's loneliness. The wind and its power interested him, yes, but more so, it was the feeling that others needed him that compelled him to go with Nao.

BY THE time they reached the desolate area on the outskirts of Casus, night had fallen. In his deep and cold plight, Khan felt a genuine ease about the Wind Equist. This tenderness was all that was needed to fill the hollowness inside of him. Together, they entered a plain portal that opened into a large chamber nearly twenty meters in height and was amazingly clean. It was empty.

"Where are your friends?"

"In front of you. Above."

Shev'la looked but saw nothing. "This is a joke?"

"I have not lied to you. You have lied to yourself. Look again."

He looked around and this time saw some hazy areas near the ceiling but was too unsure to be certain of anything.

"They are in the meditative state of wind form now. Their bodies have assumed the properties of the wind so that they may become fully insane."

"Nao—"

"Call me Equist Nao."

"Equist Nao, did you just now say they were going insane?"

"Insane. Insanity is the way of Nata."

"I spend all my efforts to stay sane and you make effort to go insane."

"Yes. You know of the three perfections, do you not?"

"Cerbus, Corius, and Kol."

"Very good. Your father has taught you well. CCK is the essence of us all. They are all tied together. Lose one and the others are lost. Damage one and rhythm is forgotten. Insanity is the point of losing all at the same time, at your final stage. It's about releasing that most sacred to all of life and setting it free for until you can do that you are nothing except the clothes you wear and the clay you eat."

"Insanity is freedom?"

"Set free all three. The cerbus is the last to go for it resists the most. The kol is quickly misdirected. The corius must learn to release emotion.

"The cerbus will fight but you must accept, it is acceptance that is the most difficult—that you are already insane—since your kol and corius are lost and floating. Your life can never be accomplished until the cerbus flies free to join them for the freed already know where they must go and it is why the insane must realize that sanity is the reverse.

"You see, structure prevents the cerbus from letting go from fear and keeps them forever held in the notion that they are sane when indeed they are not. With both kol and corius separated, the more insane and the longer they remain, the greater the pain and disease. Release your cerbus and you will find serenity. It is the way of Nata. It is the way of the wind."

"This is not the way of science," said Shev'la looking up to see the wind forms more closely. He could make out parts of an entan form.

"Nata is part of nature. She has her own laws that have never been fully understood. We try not to analyze, only to dance with her."

Shev'la stood, head up, staring at the semi-invisible figures floating near the ceiling in a trance.

"I must practice now. You will return to your own residence. My friends and I will leave in the morning," said Nao. "Come if you will."

New information had permeated Shev'la's life and it raced inside the empty corridors of his mentality. It was the rope given to the one on the edge of the cliff. No matter a string, a vine or a cord it was a line of support, of redemption.

Shev'la, in his space of emptiness and inebriation,

felt the dangling cord by his ear but hadn't the strength with which to take it.

Chapter 8

THE OUTSIDE air was stale, much staler than when he had entered, with the lacing of enough acidity to make Shev'la want to keep a partially shallow breath, and there was another wretched smell in the air that he could not place as he walked out from the building. Looks to all sides showed nothing conclusive. He was quite preoccupied with Nao's introduction. If it wasn't for a large, moving shadow that protruded and exposed itself onto one of the buildings he would have calmed; He didn't tense up like he should have. The shadow was several meters tall, too difficult to estimate from such a distance, whose external form shifted like waves in the ocean. Shev'la knew that trouble would come again, in fact he welcomed it. All that he had was gone and his corius cared no longer what physicality remained of him. Equist Nao had been the closest thing to family he had encountered and even that dangled out of distance.

He chose to continue walking out from the building, quietly and emotionless, and after another half-dozen steps, he stopped. To each of his sides were a score of Seronian Guard, heavily armored, weapons drawn, waiting. They must have been concealed by a spell of sorts for he had not noticed them until the very point of danger. Shev'la's sash was empty of scabbard. When none of them moved to subdue or kill he knew that the story had yet to fully unfold and grinned pleasantly in the final minutes of his life. It was a beautiful evening to die. There was little noise and the air was warm like a romantic evening with his Mareenth.

Death appeared far ahead as a faint, two-legged stride echoing its way to his ears. Action was contained in a pause. Nothing else moved, not even plates of armor though he could hear the swooshing of aqua in the background somewhere. A tall figure came out from the distant darkness in front of him. As he came into the light he saw a fashionable luto of gray skin – a ventan – but that was not all. There was one other, the giant with the shifting aqua form, who had yet to reveal himself.

"Give me the manuscripts," said the Ventan while approaching the defenseless Shev'la, "and you shall live." The Ventan, likely an arvicerer by Shev'la's estimates, came up calm and comfortable like a politician to a stadium of supporters. "That is all that I want." Silence came then beckoned a response.

"Is that all you want?" said Khan, sarcastically.

"Do not play with me, Khan. Do not play. I have no ear for play. Give me the manuscripts and you shall live through this night. Live so that your family will live."

Khan grunted a laugh. "My family...yes, yes my family." He decided to be direct and honest in the last few minutes of his life. Games were time wasters. "The manuscripts have been stolen—I do not have them."

"Where have you put them?"

"I said that they were stolen. Find the thief and you have better chance at getting them."

The giant shadow moved from its position. An oversized Malkar made of hardened aqua showed its ugly face. Its smell was foul as rancid aqua pickled with waste. "Meet Hydus." He had not seen or heard of one since Zorath leveled his residence. Its presence certified oratic forces at play on the planet. Khan lost further interest, further hope. The well of hope was running dry, and with it, his caring.

"Your friends are sure ugly, Ventan. Is it your lover by chance? If you're asking for my permission, I would say sure. Anything goes now, doesn't it?"

Hydus approached Shev'la loud and deliberate, but he did not wait to die. Fear tore through Khan's cerbind. A primal fear on the outskirts of death and it fed his cynicism. He, a half-shadow of his former self, ran back screaming for Nao. The aqua Malkar reached out a hand, morphed it into a wave and encased the tiny prey in a thick aqua gel. Khan fell to the ground drowning in a sphere of coagulation. By the time the aqua evaporated by a spell from the ventan's hand, Shev'la had nearly suffocated and coughed up aqua goop. He wanted to call Nao but had neither the strength nor the voice to do so. And no longer the desire to live. As all life had an end and a beginning he would be happy to skip the remainder of his misery so that he might enjoy his finale. At last the instant had arrived. Death would not be bright.

"You need so many against me..." said Khan, staring at the ventan.

"Tell me where the manuscripts are or I will pluck your cerbind piece-by-piece and feed it to you," said the arvicerer.

"I do not know. Pluck as you will," said Khan, no longer willing to fight the impossible. He did not care if he lived, but cared how he died.

"Then the seed of Tulai shall die. Your family was cursed by your father's desires."

"It is odd to me that so many know of my family—"

Suddenly, a voice yelled out as the ventan raised his hand for a spell. "He has not what you seek!" Nao approached, dressed as before. He meant to come sooner but the others disagreed.

"You will now die with him," replied the ventan.

"There is no need for death. He does not have what you want."

"Hydus." The Malkar stepped in the center again, the armed lutos moved to the background as if they knew what would happen. Shev'la looked on afraid that another would die in vain.

"There is no need to intervene..." Khan started but whose voice was washed out by the giant Malkar.

"Only ceramic. Wash ceramic," said Hydus in gutra.

The Malkar's arms rose up and from them a wave of aqua with a torrential force behind it came straight at Nao. He did not move until the wave had nearly hit at which point the water turned, spinning in all directions and hitting all of those present except Nao who was the only dry one. Hydus struck again this time with a fall of aqua that would drown a ship and still the hurricane was returned. Another attack, stronger than the last, on Nao only fell upon his opponents. When all the aqua had finally settled, upon the wet street were strewn about in complete disarray the previous score of armored guards. Many choked on aqua, ten lay down with snapped limbs, and three had died of broken necks. The ventan was not so easily unbalanced, protected by a short wall of impenetrable force; aqua droplets beaded off his tense face.

"Stop!" said the ventan to Hydus. "Tell me your name—before I kill you."

"I am Nao. You will not kill me."

"Know this, Nao. Know that Raknor the Arvicerer was your end," he said, moving his arms up and extending his hands to shape the arvicity

once again. The spell struck Nao's body and entered
inside of him. He dropped, struggled with it, milk
came out his mouth, before he recomposed himself
and cast out a wave of wind that Raknor could not
defend against. He flew backwards head first into a
wall and blacked out by the hard blow to his head.
Hydus reacted but Nao was ready and with a
powerful twist spun the unearthly Malkar into a
nearby building several hundred meters away. In
front of him looked the remains of a small war
skirmish. Only the disheveled Nao stood. He ran to
Shev'la who had been behind the Equist the entire
time, at Nao's planning.

"We must go," he said, without the sound of
desperation or excitement.

Shev'la was still in shock and could not believe
what was happening. "Go where? I was ready to die.
My fuse. It is extinguished."

"Come with us and you will see tomorrow."

"There is no tomorrow. All my tomorrows are
here now," said Khan, decided on his future.

He could see the stirring of the remaining guards.
Raknor was moving over by the wall. Left without
choice, he struck the stubborn Shev'la and stole him
away in a gust of wind.

Raknor, aided by spells, awoke. He stepped
through the broken guard ranks splashing as he
walked through deep puddles of putrid aqua. Hydus
erupted from several buildings behind. The
arvicerer turned around and continued his splashing
until he had walked far enough away from the wet

devastation leaving the guards to tend to their own body count.

OPUS AND ora collided during the time of battle between Nivators and Seragons causing deep fluctuations in regions where the planet was in danger of separation. Nata was born during the time of the greatest fluctuation of all to keep all forces together through her shifts. She assumed the position as a governor of balance. And while Niva cast its icy shadows in the lakes and mountains, Nata continued unbound and serene. The wind kept things together and yet still apart; it was neither here nor there. Everywhere.

Disciples of the wind followed Nata and trained to assume her abilities though the final path was in the cerbind. It could be believed that the cerbind was the portal between the cosmic and the real. Any who chose to follow Nata might have indeed died of insanity, the separation of their cerbind, the most painful of all deaths for there was little defense against it. And once complete could not be returned to any side.

Nine wind disciples sat casually on the edge of a cliff. All looked similar and had lost their names many tios before. Names were the ways of ora, they believed. Only Nao remembered his name. His only friends would say that he was waiting for something that would recognize him. Nao reasoned that he wanted to keep some connection to society. In either excuse, they did not cerbind. All were Equists and had reached the highest stage in the land. The final stage challenged them, the stage after the three perfections were released. It was said that Nata would grant them immortality. A more profound reason had instigated such a calling. And they had formed together to reach that goal in the canyons.

Far off into the distance was Canyon d'Altu, the birth of the Formless Fist, founded by Pri·im the Insane. He was the first to reach Nata and the first to die from her influence.

"He cannot travel with us," said one voice.

"No," agreed another.

"He must go back," said another voice.

"He will be killed. It is not his time yet to die. I have been told this by Pri·im before he left us," said Nao.

"Pri·im was already insane then."

"No, he had achieved the highest state."

"Then how did he die?"

"That I do not know—enough of this—he must travel with us until he is ready."

"Then you will prepare him."

"I will," replied Nao.

"He cannot be prepared."

"Yes, the seed is sideless inside. It is neither bright nor dark nor gray."

"Mother has told me, he must be taught," said Nao.

"Do not let him influence your own preparation, Nao."

Still half unconscious, Shev'la's eyes began to shake and he could once again hear the world outside. He was not happy about this fact. Whispered talk was off to one side.

"I will be watchful of this," replied Nao.

"The Ice King's influence grows in every part of Seranor."

"Danger has fallen upon the land—upon us."

"Khan's father found the Nivian and raised him," said Nao.

"Then he is like his father."

"No, he is like the Nivian."

Momentary silence.

"Zorath will know this."

"No," replied Nao.

"He will find out."

"He is busy with the land…" They all suddenly stopped as they heard Khan's movements on the dry clay. Nao walked over.

"You are alive, Khan."

"Yes. Still."

"Good. Come eat with us," Nao smiled and behind his wide brim of joy hid a truth that would one day be found and in its finding make freedom once again.

Weeks passed by uneventfully and Khan grew used to Nao calling him by this name. The nameless others rarely spoke to him. Clay variety was limited and supplemented with rich sources of aqua far more nutritious than any he had found. He soon adapted to it and enjoyed its flavor. Everyday Nao had instructed him to do certain tasks and having nothing else to do he enjoyed the feeling of being useful again. All of life's uselessness was drained from him. More weeks passed and he felt stronger and more comfortable with his situation. The Equists would often leave together to go into the canyon and practice their meditation. Khan was forbidden to go and as much as he hated it he respected Nao for saving his life twice over. Instead, he trained when Nao commanded. Meditation became his daily routine, physical strengthening his habit and determination to live his purpose. Khan's body formed itself supple and strong like the trunk of a twisted cora tree.

Seven hundred and twenty one months expired.

Khan could not help but think about Zorath and what his influence had done to Seranor. His family no longer existed because of his touch. All that I once loved was dead, he thought. All that was a part of me has been separated and now I find myself in a canyon with those without names and with a hollow cause while Zorath closes his fist upon the land tighter and tighter. Even the wind is cold and the land shakes in pain. He will enslave us all as my father had predicted before he was killed. We must fight him, he concluded.

"A month more than 40 tios has passed, Equist Nao. Forty tios and though I am stronger, Seranor is deeper in the grasp of Zorath. Even the wind grows cold from its touch," said Khan.

"You are letting your cerbind control you again. Time is more than enough," replied Nao.

Each time the nine disciples returned from the canyon their wind form remained for longer periods before resuming their physical bodies. Their cerbinds, less sane; their presence, less real.

Khan felt the kiss of loneliness on the ledge overlooking the canyon. He performed his exercises as Nao had taught him and found himself growing more adept at creating the physical motions of the wind form. In seconds he could achieve the headwind, downdraft, wind shear and even turbulence; all moves to disable, disarm, and deflect attacks from an opponent. He learned quickly and after each small step his health improved as did his sense of awareness. Training became more intense after the first tio and Khan focused his intensity with Zorath's face as his challenge.

It was after an intense week of training that Khan decided to raise his level of skill by entering the canyon and joining the others. The nine Equists had finally reached the last stage and were going to join Nata and her ways. In truth, he feared of being left utterly alone and knew that he could not bear it. He did not tell Nao and by the time that he joined them, it was too late.

All were at peril because of his action.

Khan's cerbind was twisted, squashed and torn apart in the few seconds after he entered the wind meditation. He crashed to the floor unable to move and nearly died if he hadn't been able to get himself to breathe. Nao pulled himself out of the meditation to save Khan. The others disappeared one by one until all that was left was Nao and Khan, who was not aware of anything but the picture of his own separated cerbind.

There he was left standing in the mirrored corridors of a giant ice complex. And on every mirror were three images – his father, mother and Calil. His panting chest and breathlessness pushed him to find his family. Every mirror he cracked was just an illusion hiding Zorath's black smile. Every failed attempt his enemy's laugh deepened and disoriented him. The supply of mirrors never ran down. Never finished. They were endless. The more he ran the more breathless he became and the louder the laugh.

Finally, after breaking another mirror, a faceless entan came out. He was a naked white with no special markings except that it did not have a face or hair.

"Have you found what you search, Khan?" said the faceless and naked entan with a luto's voice.

Still huffing and puffing. "I…no. Too many…" replied Khan.

"There is no need to search. It is all right."

"No! I must find them. My family. I must find my family!"

"They are okay and do not wish to be found. You will soon see them again but not now."

"I must see them!" And with that the stranger vanished. He continued to search in vain and every once in a while the naked entan would come and ask the faceless questions and each visit was the same. But Zorath's laugh distracted him and held him to his fruitless search. Mirror upon mirrors lay broken but still nothing was found.

It was the continuous laughing that split his head in immeasurable pain until the moment he could not go on. The faceless entan came again. He said repeatedly, "Laugh with it. Laugh with it." Khan fell on the floor with violent spasms on his head as it grew twice, then three times its size throbbing wildly. Then in one big burst like a cora bag stuffed too far with many large black spikes, his head, cerbind and cerbus ruptured under the intensity and an endless supply of spikes came out with explosive force. The pain nearly killed him at that point but in his disillusionment he remembered what the faceless entan said and he worked to turn his pain into a laugh. And once he found some comfort in that he laughed harder and harder until he could surpass the laugh of Zorath. The dream of laughter had ended.

Minutes rolled as days as his cerbus reconstructed its pathways and networks. Special clay preparations reduced the healing process to just over two weeks. Afterwards he adjusted and became coherent as before. This time the sense of cynicism had gone and new brilliance came to Khan's face. A white gleam, the shield of optimism and enjoyment. Nao had put him in a safe cave in the clay face while he continued to his meditation to prepare once again for his journey. The young wind master, face obscured by his wind blown hair, came out to watch.

"Khan, I must go now. Nata waits for me," said Nao.

"And my training?" asked Khan, disappointment in his voice.

"You have all that you need," said Nao.

"Then I am ready to fight Zorath and his armies."

"Is that what you have decided to do?"

"What other choice is there for freedom?"

Nao steadily approached him. "Freedom is attained by removing resistance. Those not sane see freedom as a fight but fighting creates the greatest resistance of all. By her nature, Nata teaches us to be free by letting go all of that we fight for."

"But nothing is achieved without fight and determination."

"You live in deficiency, still. For you to have, another must not. For you to have more, another must have less. You have created this struggle. You have taken away your own freedom."

"Zorath will enslave us all if we do not fight."

"Fight him and he will become more powerful. Hurt him and he will grow stronger until all the resistance of Seranor is weakened and is wiped clean and he has won. Seranor's own struggle to survive has brought him here. Nata is the wisest for she has seen all sides. To be the catalyst is the greatest position to play and the most dangerous, but trust her and you will know what is right. Fight against Zorath and he will win."

"How do we beat him, master?" The wind in the canyons that early morning were the strongest he had seen in some time and had trouble to stand without supporting himself by a large clay piece. Nao was unaffected by it.

"There is nothing to beat, nothing to win, nothing to hold, nothing to do except to remove all resistance against him and to strengthen ourselves," said Nao and continued. "The strength of Seranor combined will defeat him, the resistance will only defeat itself."

When Nao had entered its center, he assumed the wind stance and swirled high above the ground. The wind grew in force and Khan held tight. Round and round circled Nao with a magnificent stance that allowed him to swim in the wind, to surf its waves. Minute by minute his body joined with the wind until the peak of the force, that threw Khan backwards twenty meters: Nao transformed. Then after a final powerful gust, all became still. Khan approached the area only to find the red headband, picked it up placing it firmly on his own forehead.

"Wish you well, my master," he said to himself. A strong breeze blew off the headband and Khan chased it for several minutes as it danced in the wind.

A day of contemplation found him sitting on the edge of the great canyon looking over its vastness. Magnificence was all around him in every direction. He was alone, again. This fact did not bother him as before and he did not know whether it was because of his attunement to it or because of his numbness to it. Either way, he thought, the fact that he was alone remained. In the cold evening, having sat there motionless for the entire day, he rose up and walked back into the canyon. He warmed up and then set his wind stance upon the clay platform, ready to dance. The wind came. His stance was not so easily moved and he practiced. The wind came stronger and he grew stronger. Days later, he was still dancing in the wind kilometers high into the air in the midst of the canyon and suddenly memories floated back through his cerbind.

Memories of the father that he lost, the brother that was murdered, the mother that left him, and his wife and only seed. They occupied his cerbind and pulled at it from all directions. Khan focused, but could not prevent its penetration. He cried, laughed, screamed, then cried some more in the dance with Nata. All things he had ever been and seen passed through him wanting to take a part of him. But still he danced. At the end he removed his need of them and they left him, but he did not see what he had become – formless.

When he stopped the dance and landed on the ground in form, he was naked. His clothes were torn and scattered across the canyon and had degraded into the land. Striations ran across his now muscular body that were once not there. The sparkle in his eyes had returned but there was something else inside that cast a darker shadow. It was a haze.

Nothing else occupied his cerbind except Casus. A failed youth waited. Zorath had been washed from his thoughts and he no longer desired to fight against him. It was not his responsibility. The Nivian had been the cause of his life's pain and now he wanted to remember what life's pleasures tasted like. He wanted to once again enjoy his own freedom and to live once again the adventures he missed.

Khan would return to Casus. After 40 tios things would be different. Much different.

Chapter 9

FOUR DARKLY cloaked figures crawled stealthily up a black rope to an open window on the fourth floor of an inn. They were fast and efficient wearing little or no armor and carrying one large weapon each that was seen sticking out of their clothing. A heavy but compact storage chest tied to a thinner supplementary rope to the side was quickly hauled up after the first figure landed. Once all inside, they removed their gray cloaks and placed the naked chest on the single bed. Thryn Palin-Lorn, Rol "Brak" Braktul, Calwindellan "Calwin" Leath, and Shev'la Khan all stood around an ornately carved locked chest.

"This is success!" said the lightly armored Thryn. Two black-handled batiers hung loosely on his hips. They were a pair. "This is pure elemental success!"

The four of them removed their gloves. Khan looked surprised that he only had one glove but then put the matter aside for the time being.

"For once you are right," Khan said. "Tard head."

"Yeah Thryn, nice insider playing," said Calwin. It didn't matter what she said or didn't say as her curvaceous body and fluidic movements distracted even the most well focused. Thryn paused to admire.

"It's all in the elbow! Do you see that Brak, is this wealth or is this zorn waiting to be given?" Thryn raised a heavy bag of crystalloids from the chest. They were cut in hand-sized and oddly-shaped chunks with tiny holes like filters all over them. "We can make a lot of zorn from these energy crystalloids."

"Farcking excellent! Sweeter than a shipload of raw bosoms," said Brak.

"As if you've ever had so many," said Calwin, not embarrassed by such vulgar talk.

"Oh yeah!" he replied. "I've rubbed—"

"Where's Griz?" Thryn asked, shifting to a disgruntled look on his face.

"He's loading up in the tavern," Khan replied.

"That mute farck almost got us killed. You have to do something about his armor," Thryn said.

"He never removes it," Khan said. "What do you expect from such a hulk. He has a limited but useful number of skills."

"He's like a Serag wearing plate! How are we supposed to walk quietly in the night when armor head is waking the whole urba? Someone has to talk with him."

"We got the chest didn't we? If Griz didn't hack those two guards, we might not have made it out so quickly. He's our anchor." Khan chose not to enter talk about their mutual trust and showed just how much he valued it. Thryn Palin-Lorn turned his attention to the chest.

"Griz is pretty farcking Griz! Shat, he nearly hacked them each into three pieces. Dead is farcking dead, but that luto is farcking Griz," said Brak.

"Shat, that bony arvicerer is probably eating his arm thinking just what happened," said Thryn, changing his attention once again. "He'll never know what happened."

"If he did, he'd have us farck a shipload of morb," added Brak.

"Can we continue?! We're not finished. Brak, help me with this chest," said Khan. Brak and Khan moved the chest into the closet. "Did you see my glove?"

"Farck no—Let's chug some primo!" said Brak. "Time to get elemental!"

"We'll meet you all in a little," said Khan, while grabbing Calwin. "Tell Griz – if you see him – that I will come down in a hour," his eyes caught Calwin's. "—or two."

Calwindellan was the first entan he looked for when he returned to Casus as she had been the only

one who had been kind to him when he had gotten
sick after losing Boon, the map-masked thief, in the
street. Khan found her again, charmed her with his
magnificent dreams, and they had remained
together ever since.

Before adjusting to the horizontal position, he
searched again for his glove, Calwin had to forcibly
stop him before they made passionate love together.
The image of an angry Raknor holding his glove
faded after the first prolonged kiss. He hoped that
Raknor had forgotten about him.

Brak and Thryn met up with Griz who no longer
wore eye glasses and; instead, just kept his helm on.
They remained in the downstairs tavern at an
extended table. Primo was on special: free drinks for
the first hour.

FOR THE past 28 tios since his return, Khan had
been hanging around several groups of ambitious
adventurers. He first made friends with a bunch of
seedlings whose grandiose talk intrigued him only to
later discover that it was just talk and nothing more.
Other dreamy adventurers came his way and he
usually found himself leading the uninitiated rather
than working in cooperation. He occasionally found
work in translating old carvings and such work
which provided him with some steady life, far from
the riches he had planned. His name as a competent
translator and worker of codes spread around the
urba and he managed to keep a schedule to maintain

his wind skills and primarily trained in secret. Khan remained happy, in fact happier than most. He was a survivor. He had cheated death where his dear family had not. And though he thought of them once in a while he acknowledged that few tears had been released since their demise and may have been brewing within him.

Most of the wanna-be adventurers were not friends, but thirty-three months ago he met Thryn and Brak. Thryn was an unrefined thief who had similar dreams of wealth. His friend Brak was an under-intelligent fighter who stormed around wielding a large war hammer. They worked well together and after several smaller escapades, mostly successful, they hung around more often. Calwin didn't seem to mind the adventures as long as it earned them wealth for their troubles. Her arvic talents were sufficient enough and balanced the multiple skills of the group. And Griz finally left Tri and without anything to do decided to work alongside Khan who had demonstrated a unique understanding of him that others could not seem to penetrate. It turned out that Griz, despite his brutality, became very loyal as a friend.

This last group – Thryn, Brak, Griz, Calwin and Khan – had been together and had been quite successful. Their escapades were short, of low risk and mildly profitable. It usually left two or three dead and involved a minor amount of arvic spells. Khan and Thryn couldn't have had more diametric viewpoints. Where they did positively agree was on the part of adventure and profit. Though Thryn, probably from his life as a thief, was more risk averse and more practical than his counterpart. Khan, on the other hand, lived so close to the edge of danger that he dangled rather than stood. In the end, they made an odd but good team.

He also suspected that Thryn and Calwin were growing closer together. Thryn and Khan argued over competence as Thryn became more over-confident and realized that he could be smarter than Khan who thought little of the small changes in his character. He reasoned that Thryn was experiencing similar kinds of cerbal challenges, more related to his life than to anything else. Should this have been the case it would have been better for them all.

Thryn, not as smart as he demonstrated to be, compensated a thief, actually Boon in disguise, to obtain some information, which Boon already knew but didn't say until the price of zorn was just right. Boon avoided any direct contact with Khan to prevent the release of unresolved issues he shared with the young wind follower. Neither had forgotten. Khan was happy to leave the negotiations with thieves to his thief-pal, Thryn. He couldn't trust them and, in fact, hated them to a degree but in his new career he had no choice but to maintain a certain access to the underground society.

Working from Boon's knowledge, Khan then set out to map a strategy to obtain the crystalloids. He had become obsessed with obtaining things since his return to Casus as if he hadn't enough in his youth or simply wanted what others had so easily. The more obsessed he became the more he worked to feed the growing number of thieves, assassins and commodity brokers. It was because of Khan that the mission was successful as he was able to enter silently then created a windy and natural distraction in Raknor's residence while the others secured the chest full of crystalloids and moved it into the carriage in the street. Only two dead bodies remained. The arvicerer and Borius, the company manager, were perfectly away at the time.

THE PRODUCTION of technological devices required the addition of an enhanced energy source for arvicity alone could shape singularly powerful items: mass production required much more. The arvicerer, Raknor Valhollumquis, a gray-skinned and tall ventan, was also a numularian who had made strict supply agreements with Technomicon to process and transfer energy crystalloids. The crystalloids were primarily derived from deep ice beds in lakes and near the shores of deep frigid oceans. Thousands of tios of activity and earth shifts produced pools of stale arvicity that turned into pockets of concentrated arvic gas over time. The gas, combined with aqua, solidified into oddly-shaped crystalloids that when melted could produce energy. This energy then fed the arvic processors in the making of new devices for society. Raknor became rich from his investment deals with Technomicon and his reputation was well known among the higher circles that had grown in Casus.

He had opened *Narcophalin*, a subsidiary trading company solely dedicated to the removal and shipping of crystalloids, to manage the huge increases in business. Borius, his right hand executive of half-cerborian milk, and a silent president ran the business. Unknown to most, Technomicon had also invested in its operations to ensure the crystalloid supply was not affected. After tapping into several virgin beds of natural crystalloids, Narcophalin expanded into processing. It proved to be a sound economic move.

Raknor returned to his study chamber to retrieve a map of the central region. The land that now was entirely made of snowy ice continued to expand and to freeze all in its seemingly unstoppable path. He had just finished a meeting and was anxious to arrange for another delivery of goods to the area. This time the delivery would go to a mountain inside the Rim of Nivata, thousands of meters up. Raknor wanted to review the logistics of the deal in order to nail down specific flashportation details.

The client, a deformed entan called Denar'ka was in command: A reputed Nivaton with connections to Zorath himself. No matter, zorn was the justified reason for their relationship. Narcophalin generated hundreds of thousands of zorn in crystalloid business.

As he sifted through a pile of maps he noticed something peculiar about the room. Then quickly placed it – the chest of sample energy crystals was

missing. In its place was a left-handed glove. He
picked it up and looked at it closely, not recognizing
it. A subsequent call to his quiet guards left him to
physically inquire of their whereabouts. He found
two slaughtered guards, in several large chunks,
tucked away in the third bathroom, behind the
walls.

"Thieves. How is it that they have paid me an
unwelcome visit and that I have not," he said out
loud. "And they have left me a calling souvenir. Tell
me," he said, speaking at the single glove. "Who is
your owner and where can they be found?" A bluish
haze circled the glove, then his eyes grew and his
mouth widened. The striking image of Shev'la Khan
reminded him of Nao. It was an evening of defeat
and embarrassment from the Wind Equist. It
remained as an evening of hate. Now the young
wind friend would be found one last time.

DRUNKEN THRYN and Brak returned to pick up
Khan. Griz had overdosed on primo once again and
was left collapsed where he sat last. They all headed
downstairs. Calwin followed slower than the rest, in
an unsatisfied walk, a few steps behind.

"Thryn, have you heard anything?" asked Khan.

"Nothing. You look concerned," Thryn replied.

"He can't find his glove," said Calwin from behind
the two of them.

"Are we clear?" asked Khan again. He had been
like this during their love making.

"Farck Khan, I don't know," replied Thryn. "You lost the farcking glove at Raknor's place!"

"You cursing me you mindless bowl of seragon shat," said Khan.

"Now, now. We're not starting another argument," interrupted Thryn.

"You two have been arguing for two days. When will you stop?" said Calwin.

"Lately, you've been farcking up. But this time, maybe just maybe, you did something right. Otherwise we're doomed," said Khan. "By the way, where's Griz?"

"Brak, tell him to stop or I'll farcking..." Thryn started.

"This was your seedling," said Khan.

"That's right, my seedling. Let's hope you didn't farck it up," said Thryn.

"Raknor is an arvicerer. He's an expert at crushing an entan's internals. I've met him personally," said Khan.

"I know what he can do." Thryn smiled towards the wall.

"He can find us by spells. So my glove – you infected cora bark – will lead him right..." said Khan as they all wound around the stairwell at the bottom of the stairs. Five personal guards moved into position. They had been waiting in the adjoining rooms. Raknor's guards.

Raknor entered the front door, calmly.

"...to where we are," Khan finished.

Then the arvicerer stepped up and removed his cloak. He tossed the left-handed glove in the air. It landed at the base of the stairs.

"Khan, you farck!" said Thryn.

A short melee combat exploded on and off the stairwell and after, five bodies, the same five guards who had entered, lay strewn about on the ground. The floor had turned white and slippery with milk. One half-hanged on the edge of the middle stair gasping its last syllables. One was gasping his last breath, the other three died instantly. The air burned sweet with arvicity.

Raknor had waited patiently for his time. "The Equist is not here to protect you, Khan. Guards can be replaced. Return the chest and I will spare your friends," he said looking directly at Shev'la, bent on killing him no matter what transpired.

"Farck you!" said Khan.

"Let's consider this," said Thryn. Khan ignored him.

"Your wind friends will not come," Raknor said as he repositioned himself. "I have trained more tios than your ages combined. You cannot win. What do you fight for now? Last time I saw you, you were ready to die. So you've regained your spark and waste it on thievery. Nao should have not interfered when we first met. You make your family into a circus..."

"Shut up! It's fortunate that you are alive. At least I have changed. And, it seems, I have still beaten you."

"Khan??" Thryn muttered, unsure about the necessity of the last threat. It wasn't going to plan.

"Farck him, Thryn. He's just upset that he can't get what he wants."

"Khan the Thief? Ha! Your father would be proud."

"Raknor, let's be reasonable," said Thryn.

"Loud-mouthed thieves are always trouble," said Raknor. "I'll take my chest back and get rid of your friends for free before killing you last so that you can watch." The four of them prepared.

"Leave now, before I kill you myself," said Khan.

"We can settle this plainly enough," Raknor replied backing away slowly.

Then Raknor noticed Calwin. "And a special prize for the winner today. Ever been with a ventan?" Calwin cast a surprise spell which Raknor easily dissipated. "An aggressive spell user at that. I'll teach you some new spells later."

"Wrong move, crystalloid! She's with me. And so is your chest," said Khan.

Raknor attacked Khan with a bone crushing spell, but he stepped aside in wind shift to avoid it. The arvicerer followed with a noxy ball that exploded and burned a large part of the stairs and flooring. Khan jumped but Brak fell down a half-meter.

His next spell was interrupted by Calwins' though hers was clearly not as powerful and she was sent backwards. He resumed, stopped Brak cold with a hold spell, snapped his fingers as Brak's milk began coagulating inside him; and then he commenced a more powerful arvic command, suddenly something went foul, he fumbled killing the concierge instead with an astray gamma ray and hurt himself internally. The ray went through the innocent concierge and back through two rooms.

Raknor collapsed on the floor choking in his own milk.

"He fumbled!" yelled Calwin as she tended to Brak's dying dilemma.

Khan leapt at him with his curved bastion and struck once before being pushed away by a force from the arvicerer's hand. One of Thryn's short batiers was deflected into the wall after it was thrown, but the second caught the downed arvicerer in the upper right thigh just as he stood up. Raknor, injured and bleeding, prepared a more powerful spell to destroy the pillars holding the tavern lobby, the ground trembled and fixtures fell but he failed again due to the heavy injuries he had sustained thus far. His more serious failure this time removed both his hands in a blinding flamma burst while snapping arm bones in the process.

Brak's spell disappeared. "It's burger time!" he yelled out. "Brak style!"

Raknor rolled around in pain, all the while deafened and without being able to grab anything. He screamed as Brak pounded his head into the ground without mercy or remorse. Brak enjoyed it more than sex.

The four of them all darted out as fast as possible just missing the oncoming Seronian Guards and catching the belated, and drugged, Griz. When Griz entered and saw the milky mess he knew that his friends had been busy. He smiled after recognizing, with some effort, Raknor. Milk made Griz smile – one of two things that could – but he was angry that he hadn't participated. Having missed the best action, Griz had to chug it off in another tavern.

Chapter 10

THRYN SOLD the chest to Technomicon. This
respected tactical hand was only accomplished by
the help of Boon's fine-tuned mouth. The Mercantile
Base, a holding group that contained Technomicon,
wasn't willing to pay premium prices for what was
stolen from their exclusive supplier and Boon did an
amazing job to convince them that he had retrieved
it from those who stole it even though it was
completely untrue, and was his original intention
when he parlayed the information to the gullible
Thryn. Gullible because of his desire for zorn and
what it would buy him.

Narcophalin, with Raknor a puddle of milky indecision, was left to blame and the company was acquired by Technomicon, so that business wouldn't be interrupted. The commander-in-chief of the company remained a secret and for unknown reasons did not pursue the thieves any further, probably because the entire transaction had transpired in such a short period of time and Technomicon ended up saving zorn on their purchase with the irrefutable bonus of directly owning Narcophalin. Clean palms and better operations, no reason for disagreement.

Khan was kept out of the entire process. If he knew that it was Boon working with Thryn he would be extremely unreasonable. Thryn suspected an unnatural reluctance between the two but really only truly considered the most efficient method to make things work.

Technomicon chose not to kill Boon because of his deep connections throughout the urba and more so because of his usefulness in the future when they would call on his services. Even morb had some value. It was Boon's idea from the start to have them steal it only for him to resell it and take a cut off the top for a few minutes of work. Thryn and the rest earned enough zorn for them to enjoy life for a while. It wasn't enough for the long term. Boon also knew that they would be back for more and could count on it. He always referred to himself as a catalyst, rather than a thief. He encouraged others to rob and helped to foster profitable exchanges. Thieves stole, he helped others to steal for him and when they were stealing he would pocket some other items from the target that they could never suspect. The taking of Raknor's chest netted him a fine arvic ring and a worn cora map. He sold the ring but decided for one reason or another against selling the map for now. It had an odd marking on it and the palp, though worn, wouldn't tear. The map seller walked again.

THRYN, A handsome, long black-haired luto, and Calwin, slender, white-haired beauty, made love in a luxurious suite, two buildings to the right of the Ice Scabbard. She screamed in repressed joy from their joint passionate vibrations.

Thryn had arrived in Casus two full decades before Khan did. He was naïve then in more ways than one. His parents were from Maffin, good and kind like most ceramin but even early on Thryn was smothered with their love, smitten by it and its effects. He chose to stay around the residence and spent many hours with his mother helping her to do what was needed. As the tios wore on he became soft and fragile to life's inequities. Other seedlings developed in skill and confidence while little Thryn grew weak outwardly and became strong in secret. So it was natural for him to get things done by coercing others to do it or by sneaking around direct confrontation.

He continued his manipulative interests to satisfy his own depraved consciousness and found things to steal in Casus. Friends in the underground societies came easy. But they were not the friends he searched for; still he excelled and evolved on his plight of thievery never knowing where it would take him and what would eventually happen. Lutas he met were often smarter than him and controlled him far more than he did in his favor. By the end of 20 tios he had learned how to turn ceramin to his advantage and by doing so he had lost something dear to him, that entan touch, the love between ceramin. Still he would not risk letting go of the subliminal control he had mastered. And without the quality of love he opted for the quantity that was available.

It was much later when he met Khan and his lovely Calwin that he began to reassess in his own cerbind the presence of love and what it could do. Calwin, in the beginning, was happy with Khan who had a renewed sense of vigor combined with rationality. It was his enthusiasm she most loved and it was that, that Thryn, who could not have such an ability, hated. Thryn and Khan worked together only occasionally but it was enough for the thief to better understand the luta, Calwin. While Khan jingled with passion, Thryn played the other side and maintained civility and practicality. This would later entice Calwin during her moments of speculation and need of comfort from an entan who was too wrapped up in his own lust to be empowered.

Thryn's companion, Brak, was the stupid sidekick without the morals or thoughts of an entan. He was

Thryn's subconscious projection. If Brak represented the ugliness of ora then Khan represented opus. And Calwin was the glory of the two beasts.

Khan was always obsessed with things and not willing to let them go easily. There was a flammic fire in him that neither Thryn nor Calwin could understand.

Hours after his sexual episode, Thryn was with Khan, finely dressed this time, in the tavern during a full house.

"I'll admit. You were right, Khan. That was a stash! Shat! I've got so much zorn that I don't know what to do with it. We're going malkar!" Thryn, clashed primo jugs with Khan. "Those fat numularians were stocked. They're running in circles right about now trying to figure out what happened," he said.

"They deserved it. Who invented merchants anyway? I prefer poets, right Griz?" A hand reached out to the big luto. Even the clanging jugs didn't stir his drunken elemental sleep. "Griz?"

"Farck poets and numularians. It's time for zorn! And the price is going up. My disc is full. I'm going to buy a residence soon, shat I need a new batier, my batiers are getting brittle – look at them," said Thryn, unsheathing one of his rods. Tear marks were evident in the ceramic.

"Hey, hey. Put it away. We don't need attention. They're probably connected with the local House. At least you look good," said Khan.

"Farck them. Looky here boys. Jealous? Hmmm?" Thryn continued.

"Got the point. Have you seen Calwin?" Khan asked. "She disappeared just after we completed our negotiations."

Thryn noticed several uniformed men approaching from outside the front windows. "Oh shat. Guards coming."

"Say nothing," said Khan quickly.

"Go ahead." Thryn poured another drink then went over to Calwin, the tall and slender beauty who had just returned to join them. Her hair was immaculately brushed and she radiated a pleasant white.

Five armored city guards stormed into the room followed by Captain T. Rain. Khan, wearing a loose-fitted gray suit tied by a sash at the waist with a bastion at his side, grabbed a wench's apron and wrapped it around his left wrist. He took a goblet with his right hand and then saw Calwin flirting with Thryn that seemed a little too fast and friendly than to just be their first time. His emotions rose as he started to go over. Then the guards came.

"Stand tall! Put the goblet down, pothead," one of the guards cried out. "I've got verse for you."

Khan turned around. "With me, Captain."

"You were seen this afternoon," said T. Rain. The captain of the guard wore short hair and had sharp porcelan features on his serious face.

"Really? Are you certain that it was me?"

"What's your name?"

"Goblet." Khan turned around and eyed Calwin and Thryn to stay out of the situation. They understood. Thryn welcomed that decision. Khan held up the goblet with his back to the T. Rain. Then he heard a batier unsheathe. His reflexes turned him around in a flash.

"Wow, that's a pretty quick draw, Cap. Ever try becoming an entertainer and doing a tour?" The room fell silent.

"This is a prime example of the waste in society. Waste creates pollution that chokes our society. So waste must be removed." The Captain of the Guard swung the batier, Khan dodged it with ease and the pointed end stuck itself in a chair back.

"You know Cap, I think you've been sitting around too much lately." The captain swung again, twice more. With his quick agility, Khan dodged then swung his apron across the Captain's face. A loud slap resonated through the quiet tavern. Some patrons held their breath.

"Cap, you've made your thrust, what's your point?" He swung harder one more time and Khan swerved his body effortlessly to the side. The apron flew twice across his face then onto the captain's hand making the captain drop his weapon. His subordinates tried to contain a laugh but the tavern folk could not. The Captain's face grimaced in frustration turning whiter than usual. He grabbed, prepared, faked, swung and thrust Khan hard through the right shoulder. Khan's delayed move only positioned him to be hit again this time with a goblet across his left ear. He dropped to his knees slightly dazed. The Captain recomposed and held his batier point to Khan's sinking and rising chest. Khan removed his hand from the hilt of his own bastion to protect his life. He shouldn't have been so cocky.

"That's my point, pothead," the Captain said. Khan relaxed. "You were seen this afternoon at the numularian building?"

"There's a mistake, you ligament."

"No mistake. Jail time. Grab him." The guards grabbed Khan, wrapped a spell to secure his hands, and proceeded to take him out of the tavern. The Captain remained and turned his attention to the tavern guests.

"There are rules in this urba!" Khan, still bleeding, was held at the front of the tavern while the captain spoke. He could only stare in embarrassment. Calwin and Thryn had gone. "Rules are what keeps you and me living well and prospering. Rules are meant to be followed that is why I spent a great deal of time to create them. Without rules there is only disorder and it is in the disorder of beings that makes them susceptible to that which can destroy them.

"Remember this, rules are to help our society. It protects you and your families. It allows peace. All who do not follow will be followed and put into cages like beasts. For beasts can never be ruled and must be controlled…now please go on with your food and drink. The beast has been caught today." He patted Khan's head. Khan tried to move his head but his shoulder bled more and he had no choice but to grunt and be patted. "There is no more need to fear him in your ranks." A handful of people listened but most ignored the Captain's rhetoric. A smaller handful, cloaked and armed, cared not for anything he said and instead kept their own talk unchanged.

"I'm no beast! Hear me all of you! Rules and limits are brothers from the same family. Rules are meant to limit you...and me...for those who rule know as much as you and I and that is their limit...that is their limit!"

"Bring him!" Khan was taken out. "...that is their limit!...." he yelled from outside the front doors.

Brak was on his way to the tavern when he ran into Calwin and Thryn.

"How did they find him?" asked Calwin.

"First it was the glove then he was seen at the numularian building. He's not doing so good. It's okay, I'll take care of things. Whatever you need," said Thryn.

"You are always there for me, Thryn," said Calwin.

"A luto must be able to care for a luta. I'm always available," he replied.

"Why is Khan so different?" she muttered.

THE JAIL was long like a rank of guards with triangular hoods on one side. Cells were interlaced head-to-head but each cell remained a distinct unit. The entire structure was made of a translucent lutium with built-in flammic lighting, automatic toilet and disposal, feeding station, bed, and temperature regulators. Not only that but palpazines were delivered daily, as well as visual reports via a large photonic translator in the ceiling that broadcast live images from Central Control.

A stranger came to visit Khan while he was imprisoned. He wore brightly colored clothes that seemed awkwardly big for him and a cap that strangled his head as it contained a good head of hair. Khan had kept himself occupied with the cuffed ventan across from him. He was an arvician of sorts who seemingly did no wrong, though that is a definitely disputable remark, and had already been held on unsubstantiated charges for two months. His name was Kathar·lic and he seemed pleasant enough. The fori shackles nullified his casting abilities. Fori was a rare metal that absorbed or blocked arvicity and shackling the hands of an arvician was enough to immobilize them quiet sufficiently.

"I can get out of these if I wanted to," said the ventan.

"Do it. And let's both get out," suggested Khan.

"No, not today."

"Why not?"

"I can get out these if I want but I don't want to."

"Suit yourself, Kathar·lic."

"Who are you, anyway?"

"Call me, Khan."

"I heard about a Khan once. Heard he was assassinated."

"Well, I'm still here, Kathar-lic. Why don't you take off the cuffs and let's both get the farck out of here."

"No."

"You want to be arrested, is that it?"

"Yes. It is safer like this. It helps me to control my problem."

"What's that? Your wife?"

"No, nothing like that."

"As I said before, suit yourself."

The colorful stranger sauntered down the corridors whistling a tune or two. He had the look of someone who was ready to deal. A deal with his advantage.

"So, have any new pets?" the stranger asked.

"Funny. Who are you?" Khan replied, more distrustful than friendly.

"Someone you want to be nice to."

"Why is that?"

"Because I know who set you up."

"I wasn't set up."

"On the contrary, you were set up perfectly. How do you thing you got here?"

"Who was it?" Khan asked not fully believing that he actually was set up.

"It will cost you, breezy."

"What?"

"Half of your share."

"I'm not interested."

"Fine." He started to walk away. "But I could also tell you who's been sleeping with your lady friend— Calwin is it?"

"Come back here."

"Now, I thought that you didn't want to talk," said the visitor.

"I changed my mind. Can a luto change his mind?" said Khan, preventing his leave.

"Of course," said the visitor. "It's a deal then?"

"The information better be better than good."

"It is."

"Okay."

"Your pal Thryn with the short batiers tossed your name through the thief grapevine. It quickly reached Captain T. Rain. He's got a leash on a network of thieves. That's how you were caught. Calwin, on the other hand, is sleeping with the same luto."

"That's a lie! She couldn't..." Khan had seen them together but would not accept that they would go so far.

"When you are not around, she's been entered, repeatedly, if you understand my—"

"Got it!" Khan blurted out, his face distorted as an emotional pain expressed itself without verse. He twisted his head to the back and took a moment to collect himself. "Why?" he said with grit.

"Lutas have needs that lutos don't," said the visitor.

"How do you know that I'll give you half?"

"Because if you don't, I'll tell all the thieves where it is hidden. Then no one will get any."

"What is your name thief?"

"Why do you call me a thief?"

"A thief's tongue is always the same, much like a serpent's skin – slippery when wet."

"Call me, Det."

Det walked out and went to the back of a building where he discarded all his clothes and the mask on his face in the cover of a dark shadow between the corners of two walls. Beneath that mask was Boon's recognizable self. "Being a catalyst beats being a thief," he said to himself. "If only I could patent myself."

Khan paced back and forth. Night came and he tried to sleep but could only see the pictures of a naked Calwin in his cerbind. He was jealous, so jealous that he wanted to kill her. And he was so stricken that he knew that he couldn't go through with it. His moods jumped from anger to sadness to calmness back and forth for several hours. Sometimes a breeze blew around the room from the uncontrollable expression of energy. Sleep came quickly in the resolution of his emotional outbursts.

Calwin came to visit in the morning. She had slept with Thryn and felt torn inside with Khan's imprisonment. By then Khan had calmed down to a reasonable level and had come to the terms of his lonely existence in a cursed life. Calwin's face did not bring him the smile it had just days before. He wondered how great feelings could be lost so swiftly as he gazed into her guilt-ridden eyes.

"Khan, how did they know?" asked Calwin.

"It baffles me. No one knew but us five. Brak has no care for it. He's too simple. Griz does not have the cerbus for such things—But Thryn..." he said.

"Why would he do it?" she asked.

"Yes, why would he?" he raised his voice.

"Thryn is concerned about your jail term."

"He is?"

"...it affects our plans."

"You mean your plans. What is it you are not telling me?"

"You know everything."

"What is going on Calwin?—Tell me."

"Nothing. Everything is normal. What is it with you?" The variable pitch of her voice confirmed what Det, the entan who called himself by such name though Khan did not believe it, had said.

"You're different," he said.

"You're different," she said.

"Calwin, stop this! What is with you and Thryn? Why are you together all the time?"

"He's helping me do things. You haven't been around."

"This is going nowhere. You are always like this from the day I returned 30 tios ago. At that time you were with that imbecile Yuknuk, but every time I asked you told me that you had been with your mother. Only later did I find out that your mother was already dead. You lied then and still do now."

"What do you want?! You're never around anymore!"

"Doesn't mean I don't care."

"But I miss you. I like being with you."

"I do also. Calwin, what do you want?"

"I'm old Khan, look at me. Will you accept me if I'm ugly."

"You're not old. Come here. You know you're beautiful."

"But later?"

"Still."

"Let's leave here, Khan," she said, wiping red tears from her eyes. Khan helped her to wipe the rest off her sad face.

"Soon I'll have an adventure," Khan said, drawing up the swirling optimism within. "We can have great wealth and be famous. Then we can have all—"

"No, no. No more adventures," Calwin said, shaking her head down low. "Let's settle somewhere quiet. We're going to have three seedlings, right?" She was pleading.

"Yes, but there is more to do. You have to be patient. We need to find some valuable treasure first. Wealth beyond wealth. Something unimaginable," he said, forgiving Calwin for what she had done and he himself feeling guilty. Calwin walked away weeping. "I will find a new adventure, my love!"

It was his fault. He had neglected her more than he should and Thryn's sly touch had made its imprint. Right then and there he decided to give her another chance, that failing at this relationship might forever trap him in his own loneliness. The thought of that made him shutter; instead, he thought about how to set up the kind of life that they both now wanted.

Chapter 11

AFTER LETTING go of Mareenth and Cal'la, Shev'la Khan had surrendered himself to the emptiness that love had left him. His murdered town, made into a large crater, was filled by an icy lake: Lake Tulai; Khan's hollow corius persisted to be hollow. When he spent time with Calwin, a fire re-ignited in him, love had filled that empty crater inside and all felt cool and settled.

At the beginning, Khan told Calwin the story that was taught to him by his father. He told her firstly to impress and secondly to enter her succulence. The previous incident with Boon along with the accusations and the subsequent fainting had left a bad impression with her and so he turned up his charm upon his return.

"What strikes your memory the deepest, Khan?" she had asked.

"Stories. Stories from my master, from my father," he replied. "You just know that some stories are true. That is what inspires me to go on."

"Why?"

"To meet my needs. The personal needs inside. Travel is really the physical representation of our kol's direction. It leads us to teach us and make us whole."

"Hmmm," she said, thinking that there actually were lutos of some intelligence left upon the planet.

"The greatest story was of the binding of Seranor. Before we came, before the ones who were the first, the planet was unstable and the ground volatile from the fight of the seragons, the five cosmic seragons."

"Like the serags?"

"They are the offspring of the original seragons, the serpent seeds of the Kozotal. One seragon, Seranor, sacrificed herself. Regarded as the truest of all the seragons, for what was done to her was to be enslaved to bind the planet. Her long body was thread into the ocean of aqua and ice. Her body pushed up continents and mountains and made chasms. The other four seragons were tricked and bound to live forever as the four elements which created nature and aqua and trees and rivers to feed them.

"Where did entans come from?"

"We were created from her seed. We are from the cosmic seragon, Seragorn."

"You really believe this story," she said.

"It's our history," he replied, immediately. "Do you want to hear more?"

"Of course." She smiled.

"Ten thousand tios later," he started, "the planet started to shake and crack as Seragorn began to move. He was subdued by tracing nine mythical points on his body and locking them into position. Seragorn moves no longer. If he does the planet will quake and split. His desire has been satiated from the planet's energy which is recycled back into Seranor."

"So we are from Seranor and the planet is safe."

"Yes."

"You're very serious about this story."

"It's a story from the past. Our past."

"But you believe it. Are you a seragon?" she asked jokingly.

"I am. But I am a gentle, passionate seragon. One who lives in adventure and whose destiny will change the world."

"Why should I believe you?" she asked, unconvinced of his grand delusions, testing their validity.

"We all must believe something, Calwin. Suppose I told you that you are a beautiful luta and had met this interesting luto." Khan reached out his hand to touch her.

"Yes?" She welcomed his hand.

"Then this luto, who was truly interested in knowing more about the luta, moved in closer..." he said and moved closer. "Close enough so as to kiss her."

"And then?"

"Then the luta looked into his eyes and felt passion." Nose to nose they faced each other. "He saw the luta's desire and, and..." Khan kissed her passionately and she enjoyed it. They kissed some more before he entered her and erupted her body's sexual storehouse.

CALWIN RETURNED to her room after leaving the central jail. She sat stupefied on her bed. Felt torn by the wait and the wallowing that accompanied her. She loved Khan for what he was and hated him for what he was yet to be. And these contradictions occupied her emotions, distracted her from her own idealisms, and soon enough she would need a chance to escape her life's improbabilities.

A knock came at her door. It was Thryn. The majestic thief just emerged from a nearby room after just having sex with a busty Karuli female. Calwin opened the door. She was crying gently.

"Why are you crying, my sweet?" he asked.

"It's Khan," she said.

"He'll come out of jail soon. They never found the missing items so they can't keep him any longer."

"It's not that," she said, crying more. "He suspects us. I don't know how...I visited him today and he seemed to know about us—I'm so confused."

"Then we should stay apart for a while." Calwin nodded her head in agreement. "He also said that he has been planning an adventure."

"Good."

"He thinks that he can find a big one so that we can all be rich."

"That's very good! Our final adventure," Thryn said, squinting his eyes as he confirmed his future scenario.

Khan was released a few days later. The jail fees were paid mysteriously. The couple, Khan and Calwin, spent more time together remembering the good feelings that they first shared. Thryn kept his nose away from her and waited for his time, patiently as ever, obviously attentively served by backroom Karuli. He found relief via local prostitutes though didn't enjoy paying for it. He would often run into Griz who cared not about what Thryn did.

Griz loved to visit Number 51 whenever he had the chance. And, in-between chances, the heavily-armored painted himself in milk aptly derived from the opponents he mashed to the ground at the local taverns. Odd as it seemed to some, Griz relished in the fact that there was always another in line waiting to test their ceramic against his mighty fists. The skirmishes left him more deeply scarred and only heightened the level of his ugliness. Soon, Griz was choosing to wear his full helm on a full-time basis. Thryn excused it as an obnoxious act from the obnoxious and had plenty of hassle from handling the other rude fighter, Brak.

THREE WEEKS passed uneventfully except for several heated arguments between Khan and Thryn. The latter managed to smooth out the arguments with soft talk. Their relationship had stabilized over the last couple of days in anticipation to Khan's new find. He told Thryn to meet him at the Ice Scabbard in the evening.

"I found something," said Khan. "There's a special mission that requires four or five able-bodied adventurers to explore an underground dungeon. All expenses are paid and the only thing to do is to report the details we find. Any objects or treasure is ours to keep."

"A dungeon. Think about it…" replied Thryn, thoroughly disinterested in the idea of possibly finding something. It wasn't worth the risk. Khan had the opposite opinion. "Why would someone bury treasure in a dungeon? It's an oxymoron. Dungeon and treasure don't go together."

"It's not stupid. Dungeons have all kinds of things. And think about this—Whatever we find we keep!"

"Yeah, maybe we find nothing," said Thryn.

"It's open-ended."

"I think we should go to the hill caves to find those lost arvicians. Farck—Think about that. A party with two powerful arvicians. No one comes out. Shat, they must have some powerful devices with them. Calwin would agree to something like that, but a dungeon without any confirmation of anything..." Khan focused on Thryn's lips as he mentioned her name.

"Calwin would like the idea? What about Brak and Griz?" Khan said.

"They don't care. Just like all fighters. All they want is to farcking kill ceramin. That's all they know. Shat, they're more scared than any of us but all they know is how to murder. That's all."

"That's all they've learned. Given people like you, no wonder."

"Farck them! Listen, I mean nothing bad but if Brak was dead I wouldn't give a Serag's dick. You know?"

"Have another drink, it may clear the mud hole in your head." They toasted together. A tall, handsome luto walked in, dressed in expensive clothes and wearing round blue glasses, not like the cult Griz once followed, masterful in design with exquisite yet highly refined in taste. The luto sat alone and ordered a drink. He casually noticed the wind follower and invited him over. Khan, intrigued, got up from his chair.

"That's what it's all about, having a good time." The two friends toasted.

"I'll be back," Khan said.

"The dead don't give anyone good feelings, Khan. Shat! Where are you going now?" Thryn said. Khan had already left. "Wench! Wench! Another jug over here!"

The stranger motioned his hand for Khan to sit. The wench waited. "Miss, your finest primo. And you my friend?" said the richly-dressed.

"The same, if you are paying," replied Khan.

"A luto who knows how to appreciate the goodness from nature."

"When I'm not clearing the bill."

"You are Shev'la Khan, great wanderer of misadventures still looking for simple treasures. I knew your father Tulai long ago before he met his end. I was sorry to hear his demise. My name is Ralwindale." He spoke with confidence and clarity unmatched by any other he had met his whole life.

"My father did not speak of you," replied Khan, thinking about whether or not his father mentioned him before.

"Your father did not speak of many things."

"How did you know my father?"

"We met at a convention in Casus once. He sold me his invention for mass-produced palp."

"I did not know that he sold it. It wasn't his best work."

"No. I have been successful because of your father, unlike your life, I am sad to divulge."

"There is nothing wrong with my life," said Khan in defence.

"You have been blessed with bad luck your entire life," said the richly-dressed Ralwindale. "You watch others succeed and wonder what they have that you don't. When is your turn?—"

"Who the farck *are* you? I expected an interesting discussion not this insult to my family and to me. If you think this impresses me at any level then you are very mistaken."

"Yes, in fact I do. Your reaction to the truth is normal. But I am not bothered by it."

"Who are you?"

"I am Ralwindale as I have said and I own the silver tower in the western district of this urba. Consider me as a particular someone with knowledge."

"And now you will tell me that you can see my future?"

"I see your future becoming more clear. Like an island with a cloudless sky. There is more to this life and it is certain that you want to know why."

"Adventures are my life."

"Perhaps. Your path, maybe? Or there is always another." Khan listened closely and could not help but answer openly to this strange numularian. "What brings you here, young Khan?"

"Life...love. There is so much to do," Khan said.

"What is it you want to do?" Ralwindale asked.

"Many things."

"For instance?"

"Discover treasure. Find items of power. See what is out there. Test my ability in the real. Doesn't everyone?" Khan said.

"Not everyone shares your enthusiasm for life," replied Ralwindale.

Khan: "Live the adventure of what life was meant for."

Ralwindale: "To what end?"

Khan: "To change the planet."

Ralwindale: "You are skilled in battle, yes?"

Khan: "Of course."

Ralwindale: "You have a special weapon: A bastion."

Khan: "From my seedhood."

"But don't you want more?" asked Ralwindale. "An arvic batier that powers your body perhaps. Greater power than any can accomplish normally." Ralwindale gestured with his left hand and the flamma lighting dimmed, ever so perceptibly, in the entire tavern. Most were too busy to notice. "Raise your thoughts and all will be yours. Isn't that what people want. Power. Pure." Ralwindale clenched his open hand into a fist, mesmerizing his young guest.

"Yes. Power." Khan's face lit up and a sparkle shined in his glossy eyes. "It is only granted to some."

"Not true. I can show you that power." Ralwindale touched him. Khan relaxed into a dreamy state.

"Come, Khan!" yelled a voice from across the room-filled tavern. It was Griz. He had found his way after his stay with his prostitute of choice. He yelled again to his only friend who didn't seem to hear him. "Come, Khan!"

"It is a dream I have," said Khan. Finally, Griz jumped up with both arms in the air, full helm and all. Another adventurer-type started arguing with him.

"Dreams can be real. Find the Inist Islands for a treasure trove wilder than you can imagine—A friend of yours?" said Ralwindale.

Khan's gaze returned to normal. "Uh? Yeah, he is and he's always over the edge."

"Have you been together long?"

"Twenty tios now along with some others."

"And what have you found?"

"Never anything grand or wild," said the young wind follower. "But I feel my luck is changing. Inist Islands, interesting—Griz calm down!"

"I'd be careful. Friends are few and not where you think they are. Take this special tard. If you want to reach me just call the command. If you want to be compensated well for your missions come and find me," said Ralwindale, handing him the octagonal device. It had two faces, one white and one black. "The black side is a wealth locator, it will help you to locate the greatest wealth at Inist only, that is, of course, if you decide to go. Keep it all the same, as you wish."

Griz went face-to-face with a heavy-set fighter.

"Griz! Calm down! Griz!" Khan got up.

"Excuse me but my friend... I'll remember that, Inist, thanks... erh... Ralwindale."

"Not necessary."

Khan turned to Griz's direction. "Griz! Hang on, I'm coming." Then he turned back to Ralwindale. "Why did you find....?" The richly-dressed stranger was gone. Khan shook his head in slight disbelief and dashed over to help Griz. He arrived between them still looking around the tavern to find the numularian. He had completely vanished. Was he ever there at all? he wondered but the two-faced tard was in his hand.

"Your fat friend is finished!" roared the big luto.

"Let me talk to him. Griz sit down. Thryn. Sit," said Khan, interjecting.

"Farck that! This two-legged tree has a real problem," said Griz.

"No problems. No problems. You DID interrupt my meeting," said the luto.

"You twisted shat. Farck your meeting. Next time..." started Griz.

"Next time. What about this time, you rock-skulled overgrown morb? Why don't you jump into the mud puddle where you belong!" The brawler attacked but Khan's wind proficiency tossed the man aside into another table of able adventurers. Griz was on him with heavy fists bearing down hard. Thryn rose and an all-out brawl opened. At the end of the night, the three of them, slightly scuffed and chipped, sat outside.

"Hate urva," said Griz.

"That's urba, you deltoid," replied Thryn. Griz didn't understand the last part and even Khan didn't want to explain it to him in fear of the consequences so he just grinned to his friend instead.

"What happened to Calwin?" asked Khan.

"I don't know," said Thryn. "She's probably shopping."

"I'm glad that she didn't come after all."

"We need something," said Thryn. "The zorn is practically finished. I mean, I had so much a few days ago and now it's gone especially after someone cleaned me out. There's not much left." Griz laughed. "What's so funny, you walking shrub?"

"Karuli, karuli, karuli—"

"Shut up!" Obviously, Griz was smart enough to know that Thryn had wasted his zorn on a variety of prostitutes and it angered him. "Where's your karuli, Griz? What's her number? Number 51, right? I should find her next time—" A gauntleted fist finished the sentence for him. Khan prevented the barrage of fists from landing on the stunned thief, and Thryn rushed to a standing position while massaging his jaw.

"You asked for it," Khan said to Thryn. "Forget about all of this. I have something new. And quite possibly grand. So if the two of you can stay calm for a week, I'll look into it. It has exponential possibilities. Powerful."

"If it's good, I can wait," said Thryn.

Griz nodded in agreement.

Chapter 12

KHAN ENGAGED himself with an independent search for information on the Inist Islands. Calwin and Thryn spent more time together. A week whisked by. Both Brak and Griz grew fat from their excessive indulgence in shore-lined clay from the southern region. Shore-lined clay was enriched with mineral deposits, as well as a viscous oil that was so delicious that its high price, a digital lump of zorn, was real value. Their lack of battle action failed to substantiate such a mineral extravagance. One round of melee combat trimmed a half-kilo of prime clay from an entan's digestive system. Griz did manage to fight in several brawls in different taverns until he was banned from entering the more popular primo spots. The Ice Scabbard didn't seem bothered since it in fact gained new business as stories spread and attracted others. His unarmed fighting style was savage usually resorting to pummeling his enemy with his forearms before smashing the body with hard closed fists propelled by extraordinary strength and a thick hide. He murdered one luto with his bare hands and dismembered another's legs two days ago. Even Khan couldn't always rationalize his volatile temper. For the most part Griz remained calm. At uncertain times, an internal flow reversed itself in his cerbus and he became another. It could be said that another entity wanted to get out, wanted an expression of an extremely violent nature.

At the end of his research, Khan found himself once again at Calwin's cell at the Inn, he pulled out a map and slowly rolled it out over the unmade bed. Calwin was still washing in the bathcell. The bed's two wrinkled pillows, slightly ill-shapen, misplaced and odd-looking, gave him a stir.

"Were you tired today?" he asked casually, speaking louder so that she could hear.

"No. Why?" she replied, quicker than normal.

"Just the bed," he said.

"What's wrong with the bed?" she asked.

"Nothing."

Calwin ran out from the bathroom. "Yes, the bed—Oh, yes. I took a nap today."

"But you weren't tired."

"I was sleepy in the afternoon," her pitch rose sharply up before returning to normal. The pitch of a lie. Khan distracted himself from the truth.

"No matter. Come here." He grabbed her and tried to kiss her lips but she insisted on putting some lip gloss on. Thryn had left his acrid scent in the cell and Khan would not make mention of it.

"Take a look," he said.

Calwin looked at the map he had set out. "The adventure you spoke of?" she asked.

"I know I haven't been around for the past week. We needed something with potential. So I found something with big potential."

"What is it?"

"These are the Inist Islands. They are a group of more than fifty islands in the southwest. What is special about them is that they contained nothing special at all – until now. I traced an ancient tomb on this island here, called Inist Island. The tomb contains the remains of an ancient arvician. Not just any normal arvician."

"Which arvician?" she asked, ears perked.

"Nobody here has been able tell me – yet." A knock on the portal. Thryn had returned. "But important enough to bury him with wealth. Thryn, anything today?"

"No. Bury who?" Thryn asked.

"Come here and see this," said Khan.

"What is it?" he asked.

"Ever hear about the Inist Islands?" asked Khan.

"Never."

Khan summarized the introduction to his untrusty partner, Thryn, the now overweight rogue. His interest was minor.

"I'm telling you, Thryn, Inist is loaded with some kind of secret treasure. I couldn't find anybody, well only one old luta in fact, that knows about it. That says something," said Khan.

"I'm not so sure, Khan," Thryn said. "Every adventure we go on you say the same thing. Your optimism can get in the way at times. Look at what we've been through. The team is tired of it."

"*Your* leadership has left us zornless," said Khan. "Now, listen to me. This place is loaded. I've been researching it for the past week. I can feel it."

"Based on what?"

"Intuition—"

"That won't cut it at this point—"

"Agreed. The truth is that a friend led me to it."

"Friend. I wouldn't trust some idiot with all of our lives. Who knows what this friend has been up to."

"There is some powerful secret that lives inside this tomb. At the deepest level I am sure," said Khan.

"Tomb island, Inist is it?" asked Thryn for confirmation.

"Yes. Don't be so practical all of the time. You used to be adventurous once and lately you've gotten predictable and serene. Stop acting like rotted cora bark and get with the campaign."

"I'm just trying to redirect our efforts so we don't waste our time," said Thyrn.

"And how is that? Has lounging around been helping us find new scenarios?" questioned Khan.

"Don't start your bickering until you show me that you can make it happen—"

"I have been making it happen from the very farcking beginning! Or have you forgotten who has put us on the fast zorn track?"

"I'm no richer today than when we started."

"That's because you're spending all of your zorn on paid sex. You're giving the Karuli's lots of good business from what I've heard."

"I wouldn't listen to a bunch of whores," said Thryn, responding more to Calwin's surprised look than Khan's remark. She squeezed tight her mouth at him.

"No, but you would farck them."

"At least I know how to farck..."

"Stop it! Stop it! Stop it!" yelled Calwin. "Are we here to argue or to get rich? Because if we are hear to argue and fight each other then I want nothing to do with you."

"Come on, Calwin. Thryn's being resistant to my ideas. Ideas which I spent the past week looking into without anyone's help."

"But your ideas are not always the best, Khan," said Thryn.

"If you have a better idea then let me know. I'm listening," said the wind follower. Thryn went silent. "Well, in the meantime, I have something here that could be valuable and I suggest that we go on this scenario into the arvician's tomb. Because this tomb represents much more than it appears simply by who was buried there."

"Whose tomb?" asked Calwin.

"I'm not sure yet but it may be that of a Kozotal," replied Khan. "An old luta named Caia promised to provide me more information tomorrow after communing with the Seranivas. She is unique this luta."

"In what way?"

"I wanted to pay her but she wasn't interested in my zorn so I arranged for some household goods to be sent to her."

"That's my point. You know nothing about this tomb or who is buried there and still want to go. Are you crazy?" said Thryn, knowing that it was an unanswerable question.

"You all want a better life," Khan started as his optimistic self overflowed. "This could be it! This might be the bridge we need to cross over. Life cannot change for the better unless we really hit on something big. Fate has allowed me to find this place for a reason. This place of power. No one else knows about it."

"There are good reasons that others don't know," said Thryn, stating the obvious.

"Why?" entertained Khan.

"Because there is nothing there," Thryn said, sarcastically.

"Trust me. This will give us what we need. It will change our lives. All of them. I can feel it."

"It will save us from this shat?" asked Calwin.

"That's what we are here for, Cal," replied Khan. "Isn't it time for major change?"

"We split the treasure," Thryn said, confirming his involvement.

"No matter how large it is. Like always," added Khan.

"Right. I just hope that you're right."

"Get ready. Tomorrow we will visit Caia."

Khan sat on the window sill that night holding the octagonal locating device in his hands. The glow from Seranor gave it a mysterious shine unlike any he had seen before. "Ralwindale," he said to himself. "How is it that you found me?"

The tard glowed in response to a call. Khan called out the command to answer.

"Shev'la, have you prepared to go?" Ralwindale said, his image slightly faint.

"We have decided," he said, "tomorrow we shall know more."

"There are some things that I could not say in the tavern regarding the device I have given you."

"What things?"

"Its function."

"Isn't it—"

"It is like no other tard, Shev'la." Khan felt uncomfortable being referred to as Shev'la, his former self. "Look to the black side. This is the location device and it uses a four-layer color spectrum to guide you.

"If an area on the hexagon turns white in color then you have found the exact location. Green means that there is a very high probability of being right. Amber could be both right and wrong. Red was clearly not the right path and could be deadly. Avoid it. You may find that as you progress inside that your probabilities decrease so choose slowly. Technology has its limits. Once there is a colorized region, you can touch it and a message will appear in the crystal to aid you.

"What is this system based on?" asked Khan.

"The locator device is special. It uses mathematical computations to process relevant information until it derives a close-to-true value."

"If it helps us through this place then..."

"It will. You will see this more clearly as you near the islands. Wish you wealth." The tard dimmed and the connection ended.

CAIA'S FACE looked as if made from clay rather than the porcelan class matter that formed entans. Her eyes were worn and bulged a little more than usual. She was old, not as old as the first generation but aged nonetheless. Extended stays with the Seranivas had sucked her youth and her physicality leaving her in a frail body with a great cerbind. The communing had drawn out the shine of white that all entans shared. She kept to herself and lived a secluded life on the outskirts of Casus, far enough away from other living beings.

"You have returned as you have promised, young Khan," said Caia, pronouncing her words carefully, a natural timber in her voice; not expecting him to return and polite all the same.

"Have you found the answers that I seek?" Khan asked.

"Have," she said.

"Then please tell us, Caia."

"You may not like the answers I was given."

"Why is that old luta?" asked Thryn, too impatient to listen to a wise luta who had spoken to the lying Seranivas. It reminded him of the lies his mother told him when he was young. She often stretched her ideas and Thryn believed them as they were and only later learned of the fool his mother had made of him.

"Some answers bring fear more than others," she replied. "Are you not afraid?"

"Listen luta, I'm more afraid of getting a batier in my back than of some mysterious tomb," said Thryn, eager to finish this meeting.

"That is the least to fear. There are more horrible things on the planet. More horrible than a simple extended weapon that can only *break you*," she said, pausing to highlight her last two words. "That which can be defended against is not feared. It is things that one cannot defend that must be feared, entan seed," said Caia.

"Sorry, Caia. We just wish for the information," said Khan. It was evident that tension was rising and that this would prevent the flow of information.

"I have been speaking about such things from since you entered, Khan. I have only avoided the details until now."

"Finally," said Thryn, extremely annoyed at himself for agreeing to visit Caia. "I thought this hag was going to ramble on for hours before shatting anything of relevance out."

"Before I continue I make only one request."

"Yes, please tell me," said Khan.

"I ask that this ignorant luto," pointing to Thryn, "leaves lest I turn him into the mud from whence he came."

"Why should I leave?" said Thryn. "You paid her and now she must provide. Turn me into mud? You look like mud yourself..."

Caia turned away refusing to cooperate. Thryn had momentarily stopped breathing and had to remind himself to continue.

"Thryn, let her talk to me and then whatever is important I'll filter out and let you know. Okay?" said Khan, reassuring him that he could get what was needed.

"Fine. But if she doesn't say anything, I'll be really noxied up. I'll come back here and show her how deep my batier can pierce!" he yelled hoping that she heard his last statement as he stormed out.

Calwin and Khan remained as guests.

"Weren't Griz and Brak, coming?" asked Calwin.

"Is that your attempt at a joke? It's difficult enough to bring a thief let alone two temperamental fighters with the literacy of a pebble between the two of them."

"You don't need to get emotional over this," she said.

"I'm not emotional," he defended.

"You are."

"I'm not!"

"Maybe Thryn was right about this. I think I'm going to wait outside also."

"Why don't you join him," Khan said.

"I will!" Calwin stomped her way out.

"You two are used to being together without me," he mumbled to himself.

The old luta had sat herself down drinking some hot clay tea and stared at an engraved clay wall piece with details of serpents and what looked like the development of the planet.

"Friends prevent friendship sometimes," she said.

"Yeah, they do," said Khan and calmed his erratic breathing.

"Do you know why?" she asked him.

"Not at this moment, no."

"Because they are not your friends."

Khan did not want to think about his blind love for Calwin and how dear it was to him. She was a rope preventing his fall into absolute loneliness. "Is that our history, Caia?" asked Khan, calmer than before. Refocused. Agitation and Calwin went hand-in-hand but this time he felt the presence of sadness. It was a turning point.

"It is a long time ago," she said.

"What does it say?" he asked.

"I have been studying it for 120 tios and have not all the answers. That is the strangeness of life. All of the answers are not there no matter how hard you search."

"Then how will you know about the final story engraved in this work?"

"I do not need to know all the details to know the story. Even historical pieces are influenced by the opinions of those who carve them. Nothing is set, not in history, not in post-history."

Khan looked around her cell and noticed that she indeed received the small residential gifts. Satisfied he asked, "Can we talk about the tomb?"

"Certainly. You are eager to go. I can see that in your eyes. You have the eyes of a seed. Do not lose it," said Caia, touching Khan's smooth cheek with her rough skin. "What I can tell you is only what I have been told by the Seranivas. They seem to be troubled these days. Extortion in their ranks. Perhaps they are preoccupied. I cannot tell. Some of them are even afraid to speak to me." She returned her gaze to the picture.

"I have never heard of Seranivas being afraid."

"There is much uncertainty in the world. A long winter approaches. Long but...necessary. Flakes of snow already fall upon the once peaceful ground, freezing society. You are part of that, Khan."

"Me?"

"You."

"I am only an adventurer seeking fame and fortune," he said, half-smiling.

"You will be much more than that one day. Much more than that."

"And the tomb?" Khan was losing his patience. He had to come away with the details or Thryn might not keep the minute amount of confidence that he had.

"Ah, yes. The Tomb of Escarotian Kel-pa," she began then went on. "Escarotian was born a Kozotal but his essence was tainted by a family curse, or perhaps fate, not sure, and he betrayed his brethren. On planum Flamma, where he was made, he was invited, in the fight for the Versos, to create the Seragons with the device of creation, a white orb of the greatest creational power. True power devised by the Kozotal. Once the Seragons were produced, Escarotian stole the orb of life and hid in Seranor's body. There he was found and trapped by Rimortian Kel-pa, a great wielder of flamma from the planum nearest its source. It was she who destroyed his essence, adulterated it and spread it out like black snow in a place between the unreal and the real. But he did not relinquish the orb. He kept it and buried it so that no other could ever find nor use the small white device.

"Many have tried to find it without success. All have failed. He who holds the orb has the power of creation and destruction in his hand. There are some who would want this box for ill use. They look for it now, I believe."

"If the powerful search for the orb, why is it still not found?" asked Khan.

"It is not only hidden from the real but it is protected by an ancient code that will not allow any of those not of or for opus to discover it nor open it."

"Did his tomb have other items of power?" he asked.

"Once there were many," she said. "More than can be counted. Now it has been sacked several times by the minions of those who sought the orb. But wealth remains. Oh yes, wealth always remains, hidden." Khan relaxed a smile. "Wealth is not measured equally by all. Much of the tomb has been explored by others. None have found the main chamber with the statue of Escarotian himself. It is a maze of folds, his tomb. Without guidance you will be lost as others have become only to live their remaining lives in Escarotian's bowel."

"Thank you."

"Do not thank me. I have given nothing opution."

"Is it oratic if not of opus?" he asked.

"You shall soon learn," she said. "Be careful in the search for yourself. You may not like what you find. What you think and what you are, may indeed be disparate fantasies."

He felt awkward and without an answer. Khan walked out slightly disheartened at her grand, somewhat unbelievable, story. He summarized it for Thryn and Calwin who, in turn, summarized his summary for Brak and Griz. The five reconsidered and, having nothing better to move on with, decided to go to the Tomb's maze and to explore it more deeply. Only the problem of zorn prevented their early leave.

Chapter 13

THE NEXT day Calwin, tall, slender with flowing
head of white and a long batier at her side went to
the mercantile store to sell their last items of value.
Thryn and Khan left with her until the thief parted
and Khan alone tagged along giving his cerbus a
chance to work out the travel scenarios.

Thryn reached then climbed a set of dirty stairs
several blocks away from Khan's inn, a look of
disgust fit his face. On the second floor of an
unkempt inn he kicked an unlocked portal hard to
get the swollen cora ajar. Inside, Brak continued to
sleep even after the portal burst open. In fact, it
wasn't until a rod of cold lutium touched his privates
that the slumbering moron woke.

"I told you to be more alert. Didn't I?" Thryn removed his batier.

"Just try that when I'm not sleeping, Thief. Octo will make your head into anaprimo juice. Isn't that right Octo?" he said, touching his faithful hammer. The war hammer had been a gift from his father just before he was killed in battle from eight morb. He named it "Octo" after that to remember his outmatched father.

"Octo and you should be more careful. It's not difficult to smoke your thick ceramic butt since your ignorance is much bigger than your hammer. Pay more attention. I don't want to get killed around you—Enough of repetitive talk! We're heading out today. Get your stuff." Thryn grabbed a few worn out items and threw them into several empty cora packs. One of them had a hole and an aqua flask fell out.

"Shat, I hate this pack!" Brak dropped it and only wore his armor and his trusty war hammer.

Calwin exited the store and Khan joined her.

"We are running late. How much did we get?" he asked.

"Eleven hundred zorn."

"That'll just get us some dried clay, aqua and some basic equipment," he said while a smile spread wide on his face. Excitement of adventure energized him.

"It won't be enough. We haven't done well in the urba and it has cost us," she said, demonstrating her sense of pessimism for their misadventures. She thought of Thryn and compared her two lutos. It was Khan's enthusiasm for the simple things that she loved, and it was his continued satisfaction for simple things that she hated. Thryn was so much more practical and it soothed her to know of a predictable future where life could remain somewhat steady so that life could more easily be measured.

"Can you feel the luck changing, Cal?" Khan said.

"Not yet."

The two of them met up with Thryn, Brak and Griz at an unpopular tavern called Spike's. Brak had to pick up Griz since Thryn still owed several hundred zorn for the last few days of visits. They met at Spike's because it could keep their secret a secret, but from Griz's perspective the best part was the cheap cora juice.

"How much is left?" asked Thryn.

"Fifty," answered Calwin.

"Fifty? It won't even pay for the ship I've arranged. They want five hundred a day plus expenses," said Khan.

"Five hundred? Shat, what kind of ship did you get?" asked Thryn.

"It's a small one, but the captain is experienced and the crew is small. It's less than half the cost of other ships and I think we can trust the captain."

"I trust a ship captain like I do a cerbor."

"I met with him," said Khan, reassuringly. "He's fine but we'll need at least Z8000 to cover the ship expenses to get us there and back."

"Armor," said Griz. His armor, pieces of worn plate and discolored chain strapped on by thin rope with a cracked full helm at the top was in need of repair.

"And I need armor, too," said Brak.

"We still haven't bought any healing or special equipment," said Calwin.

"So, we're not going anywhere soon," said Thryn.

"We had better. I booked the ship for tomorrow night," said Khan.

"Where is the ship?" asked Calwin.

"About five hours by talin outside the urba," said Khan.

"It doesn't leave us a lot of time but we can do it. I suggest we draw up a zorn generating campaign," said Thryn.

"How do we do that?" asked Calwin.

"We strike where the zorn is easiest," said Khan.

"What are you rambling on about? You are always rambling about this optimistic morbshat. Zorn is not easy anyway you slice it. I don't know where you get your education but I think it's zorn deficient," replied Thryn, anger apparent in his voice.

"There you go, Thryn, trying to spoil my plan like usual. Zorn is easy if you know where to look. We just stole a bunch of crystalloids from Raknor, right?" said Khan.

"And I heard that Raknor had hired an assassin to kill your butt," replied his thieving friend.

"I'll deal with him when he comes. Well, if the dead Raknor was trading crystalloids, he wasn't doing it for free. And with him gone, we can go to the source of the deal – Narcophalin. The company

is being restructured from what I've heard.
Technomicon has taken interest in it: They're taking
it for themselves."

"You seem to know a lot about this place," said
Calwin, interjecting between the two before an
argument proliferated into a gruesome entity.

"Unlike the four of you, I have been working for
the past week. Narcophalin is the trading arm. The
company packs and ships crystalloids and sends
them up to Maffin. The current boss is Borius, he's a
fat ventan who, I'm told, has some cerborian milk
inside of him. He's no threat. It's the security we
must watch out for. His right hand, Pallano Veel, is
of the same milk.

"What I suggest is that we arrange for a transfer
of crystalloids, pre-sell a large amount, then we steal
it from Narcophalin. I think that we can get at least
Z1000 to the kilo, so we'll need to take about twenty
kilos to make it worthwhile. Of course, we can
always get more if the opportunity is there."

With limited time and only one option, thanks to
the unappreciated Khan, the party decided to steal
the crystalloids that very evening. They then set
about a strategy on how to do it. As always, Khan
forced his ideas to the front and for reasons
unknown Thryn did not interfere.

FIVE CLOAKED bodies moved awkwardly in the night.
One of them, Thryn, tripped while crossing the
street and hit Griz which then started a short

argument and may have continued if Calwin hadn't stepped in and slapped the thief, hard. The cloaked party continued until it reached a large non-descript warehouse known as one of the crystalloid processing centers.

Griz and Brak bashed down the front doors and charged in killing three guards by the time they reached the production workers. One look at Griz's ugly face and his battle clavus and all of them tore off in fear for their lives. Brak struck one in the leg crushing the bone and then watched her begging as she crawled around aimlessly. When the others came in, Khan whirled in a rapid wind stance then stabbed the helpless worker through the chest, killing her instantly. "Moron," said Khan, disgusted at his party member's seedishness.

They grabbed two empty boxes and, surprised at the lack of security, started to fill them up. By the time that they were done, they had two full boxes each weighing about thirty kilos. The take was better than predicted and a buyer had already been arranged with Boon's help though that was only between Boon and Thryn. Each kilo was to be sold at Z900 for anything under twenty-five kilos. Over that, the price dropped to Z700. Risk of discovering increased as the weight of the goods did and the price reflected that.

Thryn was already counting the return on his fingers as Brak and Griz loaded up the boxes. As their faces confirmed that they were ready, the doors opened and a figure walked in. It was Captain T. Rain.

"Am I late?" said T. Rain.

"You're early," joked Khan.

"Early. From my perspective, I think that I am late," he said as he slowly walked in. "The take is good tonight...but it's not going to be your take." He raised his right arm and six armed entans came up from behind him. None of them including the Captain had any markings of the Seronian Guard. The party of five withdrew their weapons. The heavy boxes dropped to the ground.

"Is your uniform at the cleaners?" asked Khan sarcastically. He knew that they were here to steal what he and his party had arranged. Boon had been multitasking again.

"Cut the shat, Khan. Give me the boxes and I'll consider letting you live," said T. Rain.

"I have a better idea. Let us leave and I'll consider letting you live."

"Enough discourse," said T. Rain. "Are you going to willingly give it to us?"

"Not unless you come and take it from me," said Khan.

"Then that is the way it will be."

Weapon combat commenced and all were embroiled in high velocity ceramics. Captain T. Rain and Khan squared off and fought a short fight. Khan's shifty body and windy deflections were much too fast even for the greedy Captain and he died from two critical strikes before being tossed aside by Nata. Calwin's radius spells were effective but gruesome. A noxy ball exploded and seared through two of the no-name fighters. Griz and Brak had fun with the rest, bashing and hacking body parts as if they were making clay sculptures on a beach. Octo's head turned white.

Khan noticed a shadow from the second level and just before it lashed out he pushed Griz out of harm's way. The forearm-length piercing weapon, meant to kill the juggernaut, landed harmlessly in the ground and before any of them could react, the shadow left. Khan's gaze searched inside of the full helm, dripping with the milk of the dying and the dead, and was met with dark concentration. Griz picked up the spike sent to kill him, studied it briefly before stabbing it repeatedly into one of the bodies not yet dead on the floor, and stopped his action after the spike broke.

They escaped safely that night and by morning had the zorn they expected. Boon pocketed a sizable amount himself as he sold the crystalloids for Z1800 a kilo. Removing risk and danger was his preferred business practice; occasionally he enjoyed doing the job himself and was nimble in the night. His technique, only occasionally used, was reputed to be that of a master. It may have been why he lacked deep interest in it. Tipping off T. Rain, who now was too retired to speak of, earned him a Z3000 bonus.

GRIZ AND Brak were dressed with fresh lutium armor. Griz refused to wear chain mail and insisted on full plate with a full helm. Thryn was completely against it and if not for Calwin would have continued to argue with Khan about it. Still upset, he indulged in a perfect pair of short, white batiers each with an engraved hilt of a serpent. Calwin purchased a ring of arvic enhancement allowing her to extend her arvic manipulation while Khan had his bastion reworked and made a translucent gray.

The five of them bought tards, basic healing potions, and new sets of clothing to match their new items. In the afternoon that followed their shopping they all went out for a fantastic meal and indulged in anaprimo to lighten up their thoughts. One of Thryn's informants had divulged that the assassin who had tried to kill Griz was called Hirimo and that Khan's head had also been on the list; and that the final day had passed and the zorn originally paid by Raknor to have them killed dried up. The two were no longer on the assassin's list, but the Seronian Guard was on the search for Captain T. Rain's killers. Sooner or later it would lead back to the party and Khan was happy that they were pushing off in a few hours.

Later, the five met at the talin stables, loaded up and glided out their talins. It was about ten in the morning. The stable hand lay on the ground with a big lump on his head from Octo.

The party of five traveled quicker than usual to the ocean's edge, about four hours ride from the urba's outskirts to find the aqua vessel waiting for them. Falinquistamod, roughly translated as the "changer of lives" was inscribed in bold characters on its bow. The ship, fifty meters in length, had a rounded bow much bigger than the rest and shaped

somewhat like the head of Serag without the limbs.
A ream of windows stretched from one side to the
other. At the top sat the bridge. Its main hull was
cylindrical in shape with a long, five-meter tail at
the back for propulsion. She looked fast and furious.
Khan chose her because of Gurny, the one in charge.
Captain Roppran Gurnil Yune, everyone called him
Gurny, with washed white blemished skin, long
white hair, long batier, and experiences to support
his name as the best in the land, ran the ship and its
crew.

His crew, 6 scraggly brothers – sextuplets: Lok,
Mok, Dok, Tok, Yok, Rok; all bald but wearing
different degrees of facial blemishes to tell them
apart. They moved nimbly on the ship and were
good sailors, though illiterate and stupid to
knowledge on the land; they were intuitive about the
sea and would protect it with their life. Courage and
honor were never taught to them but they carried
both higher than any other trait some might be
suspect to find.

Also on Falinquistamod were the servants, four
young lutas; nameless, grayish skinned because of
always staying under the cabin, not allowed to go up,
and they whispered to themselves all the time in
their own special language which they had created
and that none else could understand. They provided
all the services necessary, including everything from
cleaning to sexual pleasure, for long voyages and did
it better than any others.

Gurny was at the short landing bridge, connected
to the ship, waiting for them. Time and Khan were

never friends and he had misjudged their rendezvous.

"You're late," Gurny reminded Khan as he arrived at the foot of the bridge.

"Had some delays. Are we set to go?" Khan said.

"In a few minutes—now that you are here," Gurny replied. "Don't make me late again or I'll double my charges." He was dead serious.

"Gurny, don't get too excited from the top," Thryn said as he passed them both. Gurny returned the glare as Thryn passed by. "We're going to be together for a while."

"Keep your friend out of my face," he said, talking to Khan. Thryn didn't easily impress ceramin.

The arvic powered ship pushed off and slowly waved its tail into history. Days followed more days and though the crew seemed well adjusted, the passengers got anxious and fidgety. Griz never removed his armor nor his helm for that matter, and after the week was up, stunk wilder than a dead morb left to rot in an empty tavern. Thryn ordered him to wash but he wouldn't listen then Brak and Griz got into a brawl, inspired by the thief's foul verse, about the matter and Brak ended up flying headfirst overboard.

"Get the rope, will you, Lok," Thryn said.

"I'm Yok, Lok is over there," replied Yok, obviously used to being called mistakenly but still not appreciative of it.

"Okay, Yok, can you get some rope? Our fat fighter has fallen – rather been thrown – overboard."

"No problem. All you have to do is ask."

"I'll remember that."

Finally, it was Khan who had to step in and to convince Griz to wash, which he did reluctantly and with great difficulty. The heavily armored fighter was strapped to two lines of rope and lowered into the sea, suit and all.

"Hey, Yok, can you grab this side here so that we can balance it?" said Thryn, needing help with the lines and selected whom he thought was Yok.

"I'm Mok, Yok is cleaning the bathcell. Do you want me to get him?" replied the confused Mok.

"No."

"Then why did you call for him?"

"I wasn't, I mean, I meant to...oh, forget it! You should all wear name tags."

Griz remained at the side of the ship's hull for nearly an hour. Thryn got soaked with aqua as the waves splashed up and hit him before he could manage to secure the line. Mok was slightly confused at his glare as he walked past him but soon enough forgot. It took Griz about three hours to dry off while sitting at the front where the wind's force was the strongest.

"Hey, Dok, can you get him a towel to dry with? It might help," said Khan.

"Sure thing," replied Dok, happy to be of service.

Being closer together it was more difficult to hide the small details that went unnoticed in the expansive urbas and Khan began to see more clearly the connection between Thryn and Calwin. She wasn't happy struggling all of the time, and getting older in age didn't help. Lutas past their prime tios couldn't have seeds any more, but Calwin still had many tios before that time though in her cerbind it might have well have been tomorrow.

Khan checked the map he had bought, laughing once when he thought about the map seller who stole his father's manuscripts and laughing more when he thought how important they were then and how unimportant they were now. He was much younger then and was in a different state of cerbind.

His dying family affected him much more than he was cognizant.

It was the Equist who removed that pain with his wind training. Khan still managed to find time to practice but not nearly as often as before when he was determined to achieve the highest wind form. It eluded him the more he chased it and after meeting Calwin he became distracted to the other joys in life which he had left by the wayside.

THE AQUA was calm and beautiful over the last two days. They had to take a one day detour around a pocket of naqui, the burning ice, but other than that the trip was smoother than usual. Even Gurny felt awkward with their trouble-free ride. No one complained.

"This is the cosmos, right here where we are," said Khan, admiring the beauty of the distant islands floating on the blue sea. The air was warm from Nata's caress and when it stopped the coolness returned.

"Why don't we come here one day, Khan—to live," Calwin said.

"When it's all over, we can go everywhere," he said.

"When what's over?" she asked.

"Days of adventure and power," he said.

"There is so much now. After this one we can find an island somewhere and just live quietly. Produce some seeds."

"Yes, make seeds." Khan was looking over Calwin's shoulder into the open sea. "There is something out there. Something we haven't seen. I feel it. Seranor has so much to offer."

"Something *you* haven't seen. You are always talking like this. Do you want to wander around your whole life hoping to find something that may not even be there?"

"It is out there. I know it." He held up his clenched fist.

"Khan, the only thing that I know that is out there is fresh lutas," said Brak, popping out from behind them. "And that always tastes good in my bed." He laughed.

"Brak, keep your little tool covered will you— Khan, I don't want to continue like this forever," said Calwin as Brak pondered off calling out to one of the six brothers and mistaking his name for another.

"Farck! You six need name tags or something!" screamed Brak. Khan and Calwin heard his deep voice quiet clearly.

Brak reminded him of Griz. "Where's Griz? Have you seen him?" asked Khan.

"He's flat out on the rear of the ship. You worry about him," she said.

"He's a strange luto."

"I know another strange luto…"

"Who's that, me?"

"Khan, when are you going to realize that I'm a luta. I'm not built like you. I need certain things."

"What things?" he asked.

"I need to know what tomorrow will bring. Travel and adventure has been fun but I don't want to always be like this."

"Like what. What is wrong with right now? Look at you. You are healthy, you have some zorn, you have me and we are together on a beautiful ship in the middle of the ocean. Who knows what we will find…"

"That's my point, Khan. I *need* to know."

"You know."

"Know what?"

"We're on this ship right now, then we will eat, then sleep, then wake up. Soon we will stop at the island and so on and so on. There—now you know."

"I love you, Khan."

"I love you, too."

"I want to be together forever."

Khan stared at the horizon as if he saw something there. "Nothing here lasts forever, Calwin. Eventually, even we will be recycled into the Versos." She turned away unhappy at his answer. He wanted to reach out and touch her but the pull of Seranor's beauty was too strong for him. It was that and the fact that after losing Mareenth he couldn't remove such a large part of himself to give to another. He knew that is what she needed. If there was one failure about lutas, it lay in the fact that they had needs that lutos could not understand.

Falinquistamod continued for another day and a half until they arrived at a small island, seemingly deserted. Thryn had avoided name calling and just called all the brothers "Hey sailor". Only Gurny could have pulled off such an efficient aquatic ride. Gurny gave them two days free, and only two days, and then he would charge them exorbitant amounts of zorn for each day down to the three-hour block. After a week he would push off with or without them. One week was much more than they had planned for. If all went well they predicted to be back by next nightfall.

Chapter 14

THE AIR was calm and interwoven with a soothing fragrance not common in the urbas. The noticeable taste of cora and aqua entered their breath on each inhalation, mixing together within before being expelled and the whole process rolling over again. Nature's unfiltered and unpolluted best invigorated the party. Cora trees, grasses, and wet streams lined their way inward. Walking through such beauty arrested their eagerness and what started as a mission to exploit the trappings of a tomb was turning into a vacation retreat in the open palms of Inist.

As Khan relaxed to the rhythm of his own walk he began to think about Calwin and then Mareenth. Their faces distracted him. It wasn't their faces but what was attached to them in the shape of robust and sensual bodies filled with primal lust in Seranor's garden. Lutas had shaped his life. He was a pool of arvicity in the hands of a luta. Now the one beside him, he knew, had betrayed his sincerity yet he did not have the strength to deal with her ambivalent progression. He concentrated on the mission. Inside Escarotian's Tomb he would find something that he needed, he thought. Something he could trust. Something to make him still feel alive. To feel valuable.

The five traveled through some sparsely forested areas littered with tropical cora leaves and vines larger in shape than on the mainland and by the afternoon happened upon a big lake with a small beach area suitable to set up camp. They chanced a rest up. Brak laid down and immediately fell asleep.

"He's of limited use," said Thryn, looking at the sleeping fighter. The rest of them sat and ate the tasty pieces of clay they had brought along with some light anaprimo drinks.

Griz, bored and restless after two hours, walked into an adjoining small nest of trees by himself. Vines dangled above him creating a web effect. In truth, he could no longer stand the sexual glances between Calwin and Thryn. They reminded him of his own loneliness without Number 51.

"We'll be leaving soon, Griz. Don't go too far," said Khan to his back, his armor now a discolored

red from two sea baths. Griz didn't show any
physical signs of hearing him but Khan knew that he
did.

"Isn't it strange that we've encountered nothing
so far," Calwin said.

"It's because we're lucky this time. This is it!"
replied Khan in excitement. He wasn't going to let
her take his optimism away.

Khan could feel that both Calwin and Thryn did
not want to be here. He longed for a party that could
join together. A party with similar interest. Joined,
they could achieve far more than any independent
who led others into situations that were unwanted
and uncared for. But convincing those with
dissimilar needs would probably result in a
temporary shift only. Dreams were not achieved on
temporalities.

Finally, he could feel that this venture would
indeed be different for how many were capable of
knowing about the Tomb. He had also been given a
most practical key – a directional device – from
Ralwindale. Odd it seemed that a rich ventan would
remember his father Tulai and would offer such
assistance. Destiny, he called it. All lutos great and
small needed a thrust in their lives. A thrust that
would take them to places they would never forget.
He had been granted several. He could not forget
Equist Nao and how he saved his life only to leave
him. Khan looked at the blowing wind with cosmic
curiosity. "Are you still with me, Nata?" he
whispered. The wind continued to stir in all

directions and large leaves fluttered under her touch. "And you, Nao?"

Calwin had been walking around to different areas near the encampment. She had been resolute in her search. "There is some strange energy I feel here." She cast another detection spell. "The arvic fields are warped somehow."

"Can you still cast?" asked Khan.

"Yes, but I'm not sure how effective my spells will be here, so we'd better not stay longer than necessary."

"Hopefully, we won't have to cast too many spells."

"How will we find the entrance?" she asked.

"The map only marks this area. But the map is old. Maybe the land has shifted over the past 2,000 tios," Khan said, looking at the map.

"Shifted? What do you mean shifted?"

"It might look different than before," he said, searching for any indications on the map and comparing it to the area they were in.

"You mean inside a tree or maybe inside the lake," said Thryn, pointing his chin towards it. He really didn't want to be here any longer. Thryn accepted it just to set himself and Calwin up for their future without Khan.

"The lake?" Khan muttered in response to his sarcasm. "You just like being a morbhead, don't you?"

Thryn walked over to the lake. Khan looked over at Calwin for support.

"Careful Thryn, let's not get out of hand," Calwin said.

"Here's the lake. I see an aqua portal down there. No, no, I see the treasure waiting for us to pick it up. I'll ask them to deliver. 'Hello, we want the farcking treasure delivered here in two minutes! Can you hear me?'" Thryn turned around. "Nope, no one home. Any more bright ideas?" Calwin and Khan turned away annoyed with his behavior. When they turned back, Thryn was gone.

"Thryn, stop farcking around," Calwin said.

"Thryn?" Khan said, seeing the foot prints then the tiny ripple in the water. "Griz, get out here! Griz! Brak!"

GRIZ SAT leaning back on a large tree trunk. The intertwined cora tree felt warm and comfortable on his back even with his armor on. He heard a faint rustle in the leaves up ahead and as he looked over he caught the image of a transparent white figure, looked entan in every way, walking through the forest. It hadn't noticed him yet. The see-through entan arrived at a small clearing where it stopped and started dancing in the leaves. As it did it's skin became more opaque. It must have been the unnatural sound of armor scraping against the tree because the half-opaque entan stopped, looked over then went invisible and the sounds of it dashing away followed briefly. All soon went quiet and Griz's eyes sunk under the weight of pure air.

He heard his name being called from the camp and opened his half-closed eyes from his sleepiness. It must be important or Khan wouldn't be calling, he thought. As he went to pick up his two-handed clavus resting on the opposite tree trunk, the ground shook. He fought to maintain his balance but fell anyway from the shaking ground. A giant serpent head burst out followed by a long body with two arms and two legs to stand on. It still towered over him by two meters after he stood up and now was blocked from retrieving his weapon.

"Murders! Murders," it spoke. It had a thick lisp that sliced the speech from its fanged mouth highlighting the ends of what it said. Griz tried to grab his clavus but the serpent beast moved to block him. "Murders."

"Farck you!" Griz yelled.

"Murders," it kept repeating.

"Sile!" Griz yelled out before stepping back to go around the tree behind him. The upright serpent lashed its long tail and trapped Griz's ankle pulling him to the ground. It immediately leapt onto his downed foe, fangs and all hovering above him. Griz didn't wait. He used its head as leverage to get on top of it then began pummeling the serpent and as he did its long body wrapped itself around him and cut off his breath until he could no longer attack. His armor bent and cracked under the strain while his body was suffocated.

"Murders," it repeated incessantly.

Griz popped off his helm in his dying strength, held it high with one hand, his only other free limb with a clenched fist on the serpent's long neck, and smashed the helm hard into its head. The helm cracked, stunning the beast. Griz pulled himself out of the twisted hold he was in, discarded the helm and grabbed his clavus. He could have walked away peacefully but instead was enraged as he chopped the helpless beast. Black milk splattered everywhere and when he was done he was covered in it. The two-legged serpent lay hacked into more than a dozen pieces.

"That! Murder!" he said to it.

THINKING THAT time was limited and Thryn was in trouble, Khan jumped into the lake. By this time, Brak was stirring from his sleep.

"Khan! Where are you going?" Calwin yelled but he was already submerged by the end of her sentence.

Under the water, a black sea creature had Thryn by the chest. Thryn was motionless. Khan came down, worked him free with his bastion and while Thryn floated to the top, Khan was taken down. His wind training gave him superior lung ability and he wrestled to the bottom. The fight proved more difficult under aqua and time ran quickly before he managed to injure then slay the aqua beast. But he was out of breath. In his dying moments he saw an anomaly under the lake and found an opening into a dry cave.

Griz burst out from the trees surprising Calwin as she prepared a spell against him and then stopped after seeing who it was. He was covered in black and smelled of polluted mud infected with the dead.

"Griz, what happened?"

"Murders."

"What?"

"I, murders," he said. She still didn't understand but was content that he was alive. "Khan?"

"In the lake," she said.

Griz went to wash by the lake's edge. Suddenly, a head floated out of the aqua, Griz readied his clavus.

"Thryn!" cried out Calwin, tearing from one eye. "It's Thryn!" Griz relaxed and pulled him out.

Brak, still groggy and none the less aware, came over.

"No Khan," said Griz.

"What's going on?" Brak asked. No one answered. Griz searched for his friend. Thryn had gone numb from the poison and was starting to get some feeling back. Calwin caressed him.

Brak, seeing nothing to do, went back to sleep.

Ten minutes later, Khan surfaced and Griz helped him out.

"Okay?" Griz asked.

"Okay," replied Khan.

"What happened?" Calwin asked, while her and Thryn released their hug.

"Am I interrupting?" he asked.

"No," she said, unsure of which side to be on she found herself in the middle of her two lovers. Khan put it aside: again. He didn't want to be distracted from his find.

"There is an opening at the lake's floor. This must be it! We can go in a few hours after we have all rested—Thryn, I take it that you are okay to move?" said Khan.

"Farck of course—mild drug shat," Thryn said.

"It's mostly worn off," added Calwin.

Griz, unable to wash the foul black milk over him, removed his armor except for the breastplate and grieves. The helm was too cracked to be of any use and he had no choice but to reveal the ugly crevices of his ceramic face. Griz's uneven, stone-like face earned Calwin's immediate sympathy.

"Everyone rest, then we'll prepare," Khan said, more determined than before.

Chapter 15

INIST ISLAND was the setting used in many stories
among families in the southern region. It was
reputed to be an area of arvanic convergence that
warped energies and time enough that wild stories
were created to entertain seedlings. Escarotian's
Tomb was one of them but the tale of Escarotian was
the oldest among them all. It was the tale of a
Kozotal who, in his quest for control, broke out of the
freedom planet and stole the original artifact of
creation thinking that he alone could rule planet
Seranor as his own. Escarotian Kel-pa, the tainted
Kozotal, failed because creation was the one power
that could not be controlled and in so trying he

entombed himself in folds of time. The tale of Escarotian was often used to teach the seedlings the basics of freedom and control. The truths of opus and ora. Very few actually believed that it was real since no entan had ever confirmed such a story.

They all slept two hours, alternating guard duty one at a time. Once all had sufficiently rested, the party of five prepared themselves and dove into the lake's mystical depths. Griz's discarded armor, broken plates twisted black and red was the singular pile of evidence that they had visited. A cathartic lump of garbage in a pure land of creation. A technological mark for the technologically uninitiated.

They quickly reached the cave entrance now that Khan knew its location, and entered its secret depths.

Khan, curved gray bastion in hand, walked cautiously in front, down a dark, damp underground corridor. He was first. Aqua dripped periodically from his wet clothes. In his hand he held the locating device given to him by Ralwindale. As he was instructed, the black kium locator contained an advanced mathematical processor designed to increase the probability of success in choosing directions, information and verse. Ralwindale had made it clear to him that the colors on the octagonal device would change: white was dead on target, green was the next highest probability, amber was 50:50, and red was definitely wrong. The colors would change on all sides including the edge of the device and the bottom. Touching the area of color

produced a faint image in the clear crystal that was
in part or in whole connected to the key to moving
forward. The locator was the reason behind Khan's
secret smile. Behind him walked Brak with Octo,
then Calwin with a glowing flamma spell that lit the
area in a moving radius effect.

He moved lightly towards the tomb of the Kozotal,
helped in part from his wind training. Behind him,
the overweight Brak wearing odd pieces of chain
mail sounded the floor as did Griz from the rear of
the party even without armor. To Calwin's right
side was Thryn, twin short batiers in both hands,
wearing light flexible armor, small lutium tiles
interwoven with thick cora thread.

The roughly cut corridor soon changed into
polished yellow ceramic that ended in a dark gray
wall, smooth as could be except for a round opening
in the center containing the engravings of an old
elos. A true graphical image of three swirls of aqua
embracing each other.

"This is the way," said Khan.

"Can you read it?" asked Thryn.

"It will take me a minute." The young wind
master scanned the elos. The visual script was of a
highly refined nature, more simplistic in style, a
piece of art, a logo, on its own merit. He had never
seen or heard of such work in his lifetime and spent
several minutes more than necessary just admiring
it.

"If you're finished, we would like to know what it
means," said Calwin, her wet hair glistened from the
single light source.

Khan used his index finger and traced the outline of the logo from left to right. As he slowly moved his finder so too did the opening move. It expanded until, by the end, the dark gray wall had fully retracted. Behind it was a deeply colored yellow wall, round and containing six deep notches equally spaced around its perimeter, with additional elos verse engraved into the material at its center.

"What does this one say?" asked Thryn.

"What it says, of course—let's start at the top here. No, no, the top is here, right, here we go. It is called 'Escarotian's Bane'."

"That's good for us," said Thryn. "Probably scared others back home."

"Quiet," said Calwin. "What else does it say?"

Khan traced the elos and worked his cryptographic skills. It was an art he enjoyed as it always was mysterious and provided unpredictable outcomes. He was attracted to unpredictability. He swam in its oceans not caring if he would one day drown in its mystery or absorb its limitlessness.

"There is some kind of riddle here:" said Khan,

Flamma burns
Darkness yearns
Lost lost
Bandit wound
Speak follow
Instinctive tracks
Touch tomorrow
Today backs
Life one

Yet come
Trust weak
Day done
Come go
No ease
Kol free
As breeze

"Wait there is one last piece here. It seems attached but yet it's not. Truly amazing work—"

"What does it say?" said Calwin, impatiently. None of them could read any of the ancient elos. Very few Seronians could.

"It reads, 'Resolution' and this is followed by what I think is a riddle. It says: Permeates life."

"Permeates life." repeated Thryn. "That's the riddle?'

"Yes."

"What permeates life?" asked Calwin.

"The kol," said Brak from the back of the party.

"Don't be a moron," replied Thryn.

"It's not a kol. The kol is the giver of life," said Khan. "What permeates life?"

"Flamma," said Calwin. "Flamma goes through everything."

"But does it permeate it?"

"Love?" she said.

A discussion came up and while the others talked on, Khan stole a moment to peek at his secret device. A white section appeared, he touched it quickly, and a character for aqua came up in the crystal. The locator found its way back in his pocket without any glimpses. "I have it," he said.

"What?" Thryn asked.

"Aqua," Khan said, confidently.

"Why aqua?" Thryn looked at Calwin for confirmation.

"It is found in all parts of life."

"I would agree," said Calwin.

"Alright, fine," said Thryn. The other two kept quiet.

Khan called out the word 'aqua' while touching the wall and the once yellow mass changed into transparent glass and an oval portal opened in its center large enough for a very tall entan to fit through.

"That was the easy part," said Brak. "If getting in is easy, getting out is going to be harder than farcking a dead morb with a small hole."

The first room was a perfect square. It was made from pure porcelan, thin as could be made but not fragile as should have been the case. It was soft and warm to the touch. The entire room was etched with magnificent trees and flowers. Among them were beings of flamma, probably Kozotal by Calwin's estimations. On the far wall was a small round portal made of a cloudy white glass. Something was engraved in its center.

"Escarotian was a Kozotal. Look at the artistry in these walls, even the floor. Now I understand where art came from in our society..." said Khan, admiring the artistic essence of this room.

"Hey, this is not a museum visit, Khan. We're here for the goods. Let's not forget that," reminded Thryn.

"He's right, Khan," added Calwin.

"Farck the art," said Brak.

Khan further studied the engraving on the portal and as he did he noticed that his tiredness and bodily pains were gone. His clothes once again smelled fresh and clean. His cerbind clear.

"Does anyone else feel strange?" asked Khan.

"My arvic stores are at full once again," said Calwin.

"Really? I feel good, a little too good," said Thryn.

"Good," said Griz. The scratches on his breastplate had gone, as well as the original color had replaced that reddish tinge. All dents were pulled out too. Even Brak's odor was unnoticeable.

"This room seems to have regenerated us," said Khan.

"More like, prepared us for the sacrifice," interjected Thryn with a touch of sarcasm.

"Yeah, dinner," added Brak.

"What does it say, Khan?" asked Calwin.

"Permeates death," said the wind follower.

"Permeates death. What permeates death?"

They tossed around several ideas. The minutes passed by. Khan resorted to his locator once again then shared with the party his finding.

"Sound," he said.

"Well, he was right the first time. I'd say let the farcker have it," said Brak.

"Sound good," Griz said.

"I was thinking about when you would speak again, big luto," said Khan, pleased of his friend's interest.

Chapter 16

KHAN CALLED the word that had displayed itself in the crystal-centered device and the portal opened. Onto the next room.

The second room wasn't a room; instead it was shaped like a long corridor running from left to right.

"Now which way?" asked Thryn.

"I'm not sure," Khan replied. He wasn't able to pull out the device in the midst of the other party members without them seeing it.

"It's easy. There's a fifty-fifty chance of getting this one right," said Brak.

"And if you get it wrong?" asked Calwin.

"Give me a fifty-fifty chance and I'm not likely to get it wrong." Brak caught the image of his mother on the right. She was wearing the same clothes that she wore on his tenth birthday, the day he had earned the right to use his first war hammer. It was a one-handed hammer, hand-made by his father before he died, that he loved to play with. It was his mother who had encouraged him to study this weapon saying that it was the most destructive of all weapons. In truth, his fat body was more proficient at crushing objects rather than finely piercing them. "This way," he said, walking off in the direction of his mother. "I'm certain the tomb is over here." The others saw nothing.

Thryn first looked at Khan and without a second opinion followed Brak as did Calwin. The device suggested that left was correct, but Khan didn't want the others to know about his little secret just yet. It might have jeopardized his leadership in Thryn's favor. Griz trailed far behind.

"How much longer is there to go?" asked Thryn, twisting his head backward to talk to his partner.

"Hard to tell at this point," responded Khan. "Ask Brak."

"We've been in this corridor almost one hour."

"Shat, I'm hungry," said Brak. "Let's walk faster. She's waiting for me upfront. Then we'll be out of here faster."

"Who's waiting?...The floor is changing," said Khan.

"I think that we have entered a new area. Stop here for..." warned Calwin.

"Yes, stop," Khan agreed.

Suddenly Brak moved ahead at a faster pace. The mother in his cerbind's eye ran away from him crying all the while and had disappeared in the darkness far ahead. "Brak. Stop," continued the wind warrior, careful not to yell to alert anything down here.

"It's okay—" The overweight bruiser, cracked one of the ceramic tiles, stepped forward for balance and his right leg fell through to the upper thigh. He yelled out in pain.

"Careful!" Khan shouted. Calwin moved the flamma spot over. The spell went out. Khan slid to the front, carefully in the dark.

"I feel something strange down there. More light. More light!" Brak yelled in fear.

Calwin cast another and it too went out. "Something is wrong!" she said. "My arvicity..."

"Here, give me a hand to get him," Khan said to Thryn.

"I'm holding my batiers," said Thryn. "If something comes out, who's going to stop it?"

Meanwhile, Brak dropped his hammer and tried to pull his leg out using both hands. It was held in pretty tight, tight enough that it slid out very slowly.

"C'mon, quickly!" Khan said, moving over another tile as it too cracked and nearly took in his limb.

"Calwin, can help." But she was wrestling with another spell. The arvicity had been sucked out of this area and she could not tap a distant source at her current level of proficiency.

Another tile cracked open. Khan heard it first and immediately he concluded danger. "Everyone!

Get down. Flatten yourselves to the ground. Now!"
he said.

"What?" asked Thryn.

"The tiles! Quickly!" Calwin caught on and
jumped onto her abdomen. Griz followed after
hearing a couple of tiles crack open. And only after
his foot almost fell through the floor did Thyrn listen
to Khan's early warning. A second later a slew of
tiles opened and would have claimed all of their legs
if not for their lying down now.

"Anyone else hurt?" Khan asked. No reply. One
by the one they voiced themselves. Further injury
had been prevented.

"How do we escape this?" asked Thryn.

"First, we get Brak out."

"You are on your own there, Windy."

"I think he's right, Khan. There is no way to get
to you in this darkness," said Calwin.

"Fine..." Khan breathed, summoned his strength,
and as he moved in, Brak's scream startled the rest.
He heaved Brak's trapped leg out in one go, but the
thin blades had already cut his leg off at the right
knee in one painless motion. Powerful ceramic
blades slid across each other under the floor beneath
them all.

Thryn dropped one of his batiers into an opening
after losing his balance when his body slid out of
control. "What is this liquid on the ground? It's
really thick," he said, upset that he was caught by
surprise and happy that no one saw it in the dark.
He didn't like it when he looked bad. Not since his
seedhood when he spilled red clay juice over his

white cora clothes. Sometimes when it is very quiet he can still hear the laughter of his friends bearing down on him and the only way to remove the noise and pain is to cover his ears, close his eyes and scream at them. It has been a whole tio since his last episode.

Just then, Calwin's spell caught on. "Let's see."

A puddle of milk was spread on the floor. It also oozed out of Thryn's severed lower leg and everyone was aware of it when flamma passed over Brak and Khan. Checkered holes of empty tiles littered the entire corridor but because of their prone positions none were in danger.

"Well, it's not good news," said Thryn.

"What is it?" Brak rolled himself over onto his back to see. "Where's my leg? My leg! Where's my ceramic-farcked leg?!"

"Calm. Keep calm," said Khan. "Everyone be careful. This floor may not be finished yet."

"My leg! Morb bastards, they took my leg!" he cried.

Khan tried to stop the profuse bleeding and succeeded to control it after less than thirty seconds. It would have been easier had he been standing and would have saved the hammered warrior some milk. Brak meanwhile screamed in pain the entire time. "Quiet. Quiet," Khan said repeatedly.

"We could sure use some potions now," Khan said.

"It'll take more than a potion to bring his fat leg back," said Thryn.

"I was talking about the milk."

"Well, you should be more clear..."

"You two-rodded dickless…"

"Farck! My batier!—" Only one remained.

"Shut it! We're not through this yet," interrupted Calwin.

"Leave him," said Griz in a deep voice. "He no walk."

"Why didn't you help?" Khan asked.

"I couldn't. My hands were full," said Thryn. "But now—Farck, it's gone!"

"Now look what's happened. You don't thank those who save your neck and you don't help others. What do you think this is, Thryn? A game?" said Khan, angry this time.

"It's not so bad. I lost my batier. That hurts."

"It's not your leg, is it? Now, how do we continue?"

"You're really pushing me, Khan. I'm like a gamma ball about to detonate and the last thing that you want to do is to see me release that gamma. I'm telling you to just shut down for a while. Stop pushing. You've been a little over excited as of late," Thryn said.

"Over excited? I'm over excited, you back-stabbing morb. Each drop of milk on me now is juicing me up into becoming a farcking arvicerer who will noxify your ceramic spout hotter than a noxy farcking power plant. This over-sized morb feces was your friend originally," Brak stared in disbelief, "and I accepted him without question. You should be looking after him, not me! He's your motherfarcking friend! Here, you look after him," said Khan.

"Sile!" yelled Griz, having been quiet for some time. Khan and Thryn stared at each other.

"Griz is right. We're not out of this just yet," said Calwin.

"Okay, I'm sorry," said Khan. It was short and to the point.

"It's all right," replied Thryn.

"Now that we're finished—how will we bring him?" Calwin asked.

"First, let's get out of this area. I suggest that we move quickly before something else is activated," said Khan. The four bodies, Khan dragging Brak, slid across until the ground once again became stable.

"That was a pretty smart trap," said Thryn.

"Trap one first, then catch them all at once when they come to help," said Khan.

"If not for your early warning we may have all lost our legs," said Calwin.

"Don't exaggerate, Calwin. I was onto it, too," Thryn said in defence.

Khan laughed out. "Time to go. Who's going to help with Brak?" Calwin and Thryn stepped back. Khan, with a disgusted look, moved up to pick up Brak. Griz was beside him. "Let's find a better area to fix his leg. I've controlled the bleeding for now. Now, you two go ahead and check the floor on your way," Khan said.

"Dead," Griz said.

"No, not dead."

"Looks dead."

"We have to fix your language, Griz. It's not going to work like this. I feel like I'm talking to a moving tree," said Khan.

Brak's consciousness came in and out. The next time he came to he blurted out, "My head is killing me. How about some aqua?"

Griz looked once at Brak then once at Khan. "No, not dead,"

They arrived at the point of entry. A potion to stop the bleeding was wrestled from Thryn's stash and was used to seal up the wound. After that, Thryn stared down Brak.

"Farck you!" Brak said and in his excitement fell over. Khan was there to pick him up.

"Come on. Use my shoulder for balance but you're hopping the rest of the way," said Khan, angry at the stupidity of it all. It would be better if he were alone.

THEY TRAVELED, cautiously, down the left side of the hallway and approached another portal, this time rectangular. Khan managed to look at the device when the others were distracted. The answer was 'abyss'.

Again a riddle rested on the portal. It read, 'Between'.

"Between what?" said Thryn.

"These riddles are increasingly difficult," said Calwin. "There is no correlation to this word. It could be many things."

"Let's think for a while. I'm sure we can come up with something," said Khan. The smile on his face gave it away. He was hiding something.

"Why are you always smiling? Do you know something that we don't?"

"No."

"What is it?"

"You are not holding something back from us, are you?" said Thryn.

"Let's see it, Shev'la Khan," she said.

There was no way to hide it any further and the danger of staying in this hallway pressured him to resolve this small problem quickly. Khan took out the small black device. "This is a locator to the tomb. It gives me directions to where it is."

"You had this all along and didn't say anything," said Calwin.

"It wasn't necessary for you to know."

"A locating device is necessary."

"My leg is farcked because you didn't use that thing," said Brak.

"No, Brak. Your leg is farcked because you're a moron," replied Thryn.

"You are really starting to aggravate me."

"Keep talking, cripple. What are you going to do? Hop on my foot?"

"Hey, Thryn."

"What?"

"Farck you!" Brak yelled out.

"What does it do?" asked Calwin.

"It increases the probability of success, that's all." Khan went on to explain the basic functions. "You see, the answer to this riddle, according to this device is the 'abyss'. When you think about it, the riddle probably means the space between planums." He called out the word and sure enough the portal opened. Drawn by curiosity, they stepped inside.

Chapter 17

SOMETHING FELT strange.

The five of them had entered a room perpendicular to the corridor they just exited yet did not have the expected falling effects. Inside was a perfectly hexagonal room with six oddly colored portals. The portal they had just stepped through, located on the floor, assumed the form of the new room.

"But how were we supposed to get that without this device?" asked Calwin, as questions swelled up in her cerbind and came out on their own.

"I don't know," replied Khan.

"Who gave that to you, anyway?" She pointed to that mysterious locator which she believed was gifted in both technology and arvicity.

"A friend."

"That's some device, suited specifically for this place," she started. "It takes a genius to be able to answer these riddles. Entans are gifted with intelligence but this goes beyond what is natural. There is no connection or hint to solve the riddles. Only a certain level of cerbind equal to that of a Kozotal could even have a chance at answering the Kozotalian riddles. I'm not even going to think what is at the end of this tomb, let alone the rooms leading up to it. I vote that we go right now."

"We just got here, Calwin," said Thryn.

"And we go right now. This thing is way beyond our heads. If I had known this before..."

"Typical luta," said Brak. Calwin ignored the one-legged entan.

"You don't make anything in this life without going above your head," said Khan.

"You will get us all killed with your ideas. I have had enough. I'm going. You go to your own crazy death. Leave me out of it," said Calwin, turning to leave without consensus. The portal was gone. "Open the portal!"

Khan stood by the same spot they had entered and called out the word but nothing happened. The device showed no existence of the portal that should have been in the floor. "There's no going back. We have no choice but to continue."

She slapped him in the face. It stung. "This is on your head." She then moved into Thryn's arms to cry. Thryn pretended to look surprised and then patted her lightly as if not interested. He was most

interested in the love of his life. The secret love.
None other could show him the compassion that
Calwin did. Prostitutes were just that, prostitutes.
Paid for services rendered. Calwin was wholesome
and real. That appealed to him. It caressed his ego.

"Go," said Griz.

"Yes. It is like life itself. Once you have stepped
forward there is no retracing your steps," said Khan.
"It is the teacher and test all in one."

"Where are we now?" asked Brak.

"The third room."

ON EACH portal was an inscription like the first
three entrances. They read in order from left to
right: Ceramico, Flamma, Cora, Arvano, Nata, and
Niva. The composition of each portal matched its
inscription. The ceramico portal was porcelan white;
a bright colorful haze blocked the flamma portal; the
cora portal, tan in color, seemed soft like the trunk of
a tree; a portal of blue and white energy made up the
Arvano portal; thick wind, a darker haze than
flamma, blocked the entrance to Nata; and a sheet of
dense translucent blue ice blocked Niva's portal.

"Where is the riddle?" asked Thryn, searching
with the others for the sign of assistance. "This one
has no riddle."

"What does the device say, Khan?" asked Calwin.

The device showed nothing clear until it was
rotated around so that it too was perpendicular to
the previous corridor. Once there, the colors lit up,

two in fact; green pointed in the direction of both the ceramico and the flamma portal. The rest were black. When Khan touched the green for both gave him the same partial response: element. The party, especially Calwin, was not happy to hear this.

"I thought this thing was supposed to identify the portal, the right portal," said Thryn.

"I never said that. The locator only increases the probability of making the right choice," replied Khan.

"Maybe you are reading it wrong. You have a habit of overlooking the small details."

"I'm not reading it wrong and don't be an elliptical moron."

"Who are you calling an elliptical moron? Look where we are. Who put us here in the first place and told us that we would find great treasure?"

"Nothing great comes from complaining! The only thing you get from complaining is that you get dead."

"Are you threatening me? Are you threatening me?" said Thryn.

"I'm just telling you a fact," said Khan.

"The two of you better just shut up!" screamed Calwin. She stood nearer to Thryn if only by two or three small steps. It was enough for Khan to notice. Maybe it had meant nothing but maybe it did. He tried not to think about such things as the emotions ran through him.

"Keep your facts to yourself," added Thryn.

"I'll remember that," replied Khan.

Griz and Brak had already been sitting since entering, seeing no quick solution to this room. They had expected a milkbath and were disappointed.

Each room's difficulty increased in leaps of multiples, more multiples than could be predicted. Khan had almost immediately begun to search for other key points of information in here while Calwin tried to manipulate some identification spells. The room showed a high trace of active arvicity. This was different from the standard. When arvicity was shaped and cast it became stale the moment after releasing its effects. Once stale it was swept up into the arvic pools and recycled until it once again had active properties. But this room, this place, held active arvicity as if the very walls were continually recreating themselves to maintain the visual presence of a stable nature while in actuality it held the illusion of all things they saw.

An hour and a half passed. The party had eaten some dried clay during their search for clues. Khan had been the most active, most likely because of his reaction to Calwin's shift. It calmed him to keep his cerbind preoccupied on an important task. In his diligence he had noticed one interesting fact – the ceramico portal was pure white just as the purest parts of his skin. Entan skin.

"What is the color of entan skin?" he asked, no one in particular.

"White," said Thryn. "What's that got to do—"

"Everything. The first entans had skin of porcelan and it was white just like this portal."

"Why choose ceramico?"

"Because flamma was the creator and now remains as our communicator but we, entans, are made up of porcelan and if anyone would come to visit this place it would be someone of a porcelan structure."

"How can you be so sure of that?" asked Calwin.

"If the Kozotal came here then they wouldn't be of ceramico," said Brak.

Griz sat and listened, trying to grasp the substance of their discussion more than anything else.

"But the Kozotal could not come here not after they sealed themselves off from this planet. This was the place of Seragons. Escarotian is only here because he stole the device of creation and hid it here. Here is the land of entans and beings of ceramico."

"I think it still could be either," said Thryn.

"Can't you see it? Entans would sooner or later come. We are the only ones who can pass through a ceramico portal safely."

"You know what I think?"

"What?"

"I think that if flamma is used for communication and travel then that is our best option. It will help us travel." Thryn had already moved up to the hazy portal. "Flamma is travel, right?"

"You've got a point, Thryn," said Calwin. "We have to travel and traveling requires flamma."

"Why are you siding with him?" asked Khan.

"I'm not siding with anyone and don't get so sensitive," she started. "You aren't certain yourself.

It could be either portal, but Thryn has a good point. I say we vote. Sitting around here is not helping."

"Let's go. Gurny isn't going to wait forever on this," said Thryn.

"I'm in for the flamma portal," said Brak.

"Griz, how about you?" asked Thryn.

"No care," answered Griz.

"Looks like you are out of luck, Khan."

"It's not flamma," replied Khan.

"How do you know? Did you construct this place?"

"It's stupid to think that it is flamma."

"Let me ask you a question. Did you construct this place?"

"No."

"Thank you. My point is made. You don't know so stop acting like you do." Thryn enjoyed it most to make others feel stupid. It gave him a greater sense of prestige in other's eyes. Calwin was impressed by it. The obvious influences in life were more easily accepted than the ideas hidden by obscurity and thought. But the not so plain and uninteresting was often the more so rich.

"Fine, fine, fine. Go ahead your majesty. I've given you my best answer but if you want to go ahead and hurt yourself then that is fine by me. I'll hang around here. Call me when it's safe."

Chapter 18

THREE READIED themselves. Thryn was in front
followed by Calwin then Brak. Khan and Griz
waited in the hexagonal room. A fine rope was tied
to each of their three waists. Thryn spoke the verse,
revealing a spectacular rainbow of colors imploding
and exploding upon themselves, and led the other
two inside.

Khan decided it was a good idea, despite him
starting to seriously despise the thief and his ex·
relationship·luta·friend, to hold onto the end of the
rope. An unknown source of certainty provided the
right decision that so tied him to where he was, but
he kept his promise to Thryn and allowed him his

predictable indulgence. One-by-one they disappeared into the colorful rainbow.

Exactly seven minutes after Brak had entered, the pull of the rope stopped and all stood still. No pull, no drop, and no weight was felt on the line. Khan called out Calwin's name several times but heard nothing in response. All was silent. Griz was happy that the nuisance had gone and that they were left to their own devices.

Pulling on the rope produced no effect either especially with just two hands so he called his single remaining friend over to help out. Griz easily had the strength of two and together they pulled hard. The rope started to move. It felt as if they were dragging them through something rather than pulling them while on something.

"Griz, hold the line while I see if I can take a look," said Khan.

He grunted in agreement.

When Khan pushed his head inside, an immediate weightlessness came over his cerbind as colored flamma flowed through his head. It took him a minute to adjust before he was able to see what appeared to be three entans in a semi-uniform line. Their bodies had become colored like all else and were slowly congealing into a white essence. He could feel his own head being separated from his physical self and quickly resisted. A vacuum, constructed of the rainbows, caressed him. It's soothing touch warmed him and tugged at him, calling him further inside. Khan resisted and using his limbs for support withdrew his head; once free, he needed a minute to recalibrate his orientation.

"They're...in trouble, pull..." said Khan. "I told them not to go. It is impossible to redirect a solidified cerbind. And it is easy to make one's cerbind solidified—I should know, but why take a wrong move when the right one presents itself. That is plain stupidity. That is the sight of pride drowning the individual."

The two heaved and centimeter by centimeter the rope returned. A leg, without the lower part, appeared first. Brak's severed leg was followed by the rest of his body dragged on the ground and not awake. Once Brak was in, it made it easier to pull in Calwin and finally Thryn. All three bodies made it back. They were comatose.

"Should've listened to me," said Khan.

"Dead," said Griz.

"No, not dead."

"We go."

"We should, Griz. We should but these farcking morons...I hate them." He couldn't just leave them behind. So they sat and waited.

Eighteen minutes and 28 seconds later, Calwin began to stir.

"Calwin, are you okay?" asked Khan, shaking her gently, feeling her smooth skin in his hands once again. How he missed her tender touch. "Calwin?"

"Khan? Khan, what are you doing here?" she said.

"We're here together, remember?"

"But Thryn and I...we were together...and...what happened?"

"I pulled you out."

"You pulled..." The strain on her head was too strong to continue.

Thryn and Brak came to shortly after that.

"It was the wrong portal," Thryn said plainly, not admitting a mistake nor guilt but simply stating a fact. "Thanks."

"Hold the thanks until we get out," said Khan. "What happened in there, Calwin?"

"I remember bright colors, beautiful colors circling around like rainbows. The deeper we entered the more beauty until the rainbows came at us. They entered my cerbind. After that I remember sailing through the air into a bright, bright flamma spot. It felt good to go but I still felt some attachment, some resistance, then it slowly faded—"

"Morbfarcker! My leg is killing me," yelled Brak. "Whose bright farcking idea was it to go down this flower portal? That is the last time I listen to your sick cerbind."

"Shut up!" retorted Thryn. "No one asked for your opinion."

"That's all I remember," she added.

"Rest up and get ready. We're going through ceramico," said Khan, impatience had set in. They had wasted enough time. "You can follow if you want or you can choose your portal of death. It's up to you. Griz, are you ready?"

Griz was always ready. He provided the low grunt to express his displeasure with the rest of party.

ONCE THROUGH the portal labeled ceramico the party of five stepped onto a corridor of white porcelan. It was wide enough to fit two of them comfortably and they moved ahead. Every three hundred meters the corridor hit a corner and veered off in a diagonal direction. Thryn estimated that is was a perfect 45° angle and it zigzagged for hours upon hours.

Thryn and Calwin chatted the whole time about nothing in particular, but they were comfortable together. Being comfortable was a faded memory in Khan's life. He knew work. That was his comfort. That was his wife. Ahead of the rest of the party, Khan monitored the area and led the group. A rhythmic hopping sound came from the rear. It was the combined efforts of Brak and his long-handled hammer being used as false leg. Griz, for the most part, walked at the back but after the first hour Khan called him up front. He had felt jealous of Calwin and instead of falling into his own stupid thoughts he decided that it was better to remain friendly. Griz, of course, was not much of a conversationalist, imprisoned by his dull cerbus and lack of skill in vocalizing verse. The two conversed anyhow and Khan gave his hulking friend a chance to practice.

At the top of the sixth hour, the last corridor finished with a dead end. Like before, a riddle was inscribed, much more difficult than previous but the device still managed to spit out the answer. Even Khan began to raise questions about Ralwindale. Where did he get this advanced piece of technology from? Where had they really gone?

He suspected that the tomb contained another item or task still tucked away from his foresight. It didn't make any sense for a numularian to offer so much for so little. What was the strangest part of the whole deal, and he kicked himself for not seeing it before, was that his father had never, in his entire life, dealt with any numularians. In fact, his father hated any of those who worked to profit from other entans thinking that numularians should use their abilities to nurture and protect Seranor rather than conquer and divide her wealth. His father was only an inventor and cared not to profit from his expenditures in creativity. It was simply, he believed, an obligation and not an occupation. This raised a handful more questions about Ralwindale than could not be reasonably answered in the tomb itself. Was this place really a tomb? The answers along with their lives would have to wait.

Chapter 19

THE FOURTH room was small and perfectly square. It had just enough space for six so the five of them fit just right, with Griz and Brak counting as two extra halves. Lining all the four walls were evenly spaced out shelves containing hand-sized cylindrical vials of liquid. Twenty-four in all. The vials all had labels ranging from intelligence to body parts including sexual parts.

Brak's attention stuck with the one labeled PENILE.

"That's what I was looking for," he said, picking up the vial from its space. "This must help my little serpent grow up to be a big snake."

Khan stared at him not wanting to warn a moron of making a moronic mistake. The others searched for something to satisfy their own inner desires, and as they scanned, Brak drank the entire contents of the vial then looked down at his crotch.

"Anything?" asked Thryn, wanting to try his own vial.

"It's starting to tingle between my legs," said Brak.

"Maybe it's giving you an orgasm."

"No, wait..." A tingling sensation like thousands of tiny bubbles blowing out from a tube spread over his crotch. Then it happened. The bulge of his penis increased in size and grew larger and larger. He watched with plentiful eyes. "I'm going to be the king! Stand back lutas because Brak is on the attack!" He stroked it twice admiring its masculinity then the unspeakable happened. In one sudden moment his penis bulged one last time outwards before shrinking to one tenth of its original size. The wailing scream that came from the heavily armored, single-legged, warrior deafened all the others in the room. He hopped about in primal pain hitting his penis in a last effort to get it back to normal. Thryn punched him and he fell onto the ground. Wetness swelled in his eye.

"You shouldn't talk about your crotch so much," said Calwin, adding insult to his injury. Brak moved to hit her but Thryn was there with another round of fists.

"Don't even think about, luta," said Thryn.

"According to Brak's test – thank you, Brak – the vials must have an opposite effect than what the labels say," said Khan. "It's an assumption but it's the best we are going to get unless we have some others who want to experiment."

"Farckers!" Brak yelled. "Farck this tomb!"

"I would caution that more than one could be deadly," said Calwin. "So I suggest that if we grab one we choose carefully."

Each of them looked over the 23 vials and made their selection. Khan grabbed two. Thryn drank his vial of FEAR to no apparent effect while Calwin finished a vial of ANTI-ARVICITY.

Griz needed some help to find what he wanted and two choices were pretty obvious: ugliness and illiteracy. It took some convincing but Griz eventually drank the vial of ILLITERACY. Communication was far more useful than vanity. When he finished drinking his vial, Griz grabbed his throat and coughed. The coughing turned into choking and then he was down on the floor gasping for oxygen. Khan pounded on and around his breast plate to get his breathing working. Griz still couldn't breathe and; instead, choked violently for five or six minutes until it calmed down on its own accord.

"Are you okay?" asked Khan. Griz couldn't speak. He had lost all ability to communicate. "That's just great."

"It's an improvement," said Brak, trying to be vengeful more than funny. He didn't want to be the only one with a deformity.

"Which one did you choose?" asked Thryn.

Khan held up two open-faced hands. ENTRANCE and HATE. If I choose HATE we will remain here for I have no exit. If I choose ENTRANCE, I sacrifice my choice for the party. It seems none of you had considered this option and without me, you would have sealed yourselves off for good. I should just take the potion of HATE so that we can remember this day."

"You wouldn't do that, would you?" said Calwin.

"He would," said Thryn. "I know he would."

"That's right, I would. My work is never appreciated here. I found this place. I got us here. I have found our way safely and you just farcking complain all the time. What will it take for you to stop complaining, to take control of your lives. What will it take?!"

Silence followed. Then, in a burst, Thryn jumped Khan and started pummeling him with his bare porcelan knuckles. Khan took a few hits before he was able to move into a better position. The two wrestled for more reasons than a potion. Jealousy, hatred, and anger congealed into the two entan shapes intertwined in a tussle. At the final point, Khan's shifty movements defeated Thryn and left the thief in a losing situation where he choked and gasped for breath under the pressure of Khan's forearm.

"What will it take?!" screamed Khan at his partner. "Can you tell me? Say it! I want to know."

"Let him be, Khan," said Calwin.

"I want to hear it."

"Khan, this is not helping our situation at all."

"Knock him one for me," said Brak.

"Say it!" cried Khan. "Say it or I will not take a liking to your attitude. Now, say it!"

"Courage," said Griz with complete surprise to all especially to Khan who had first met his friend, "it will take courage and it is what our team lacks. It is a weakness in entans to lose their courage in the face of uncertainty. I have lost several friends to this in my youth and I do not know why I have survived them but we need to move forward with renewed strength. All is not lost."

Completely flabbergasted at his ability to express his thoughts, stunned looks found their way on all the other's faces. Khan relaxed his grip and let Thryn go to cough on his own. They were shocked at the drastic change in Griz, the grim luto who spoke nearly no verse a short ten minutes ago.

"Griz, you can speak!" said Khan.

"Yes, Khan. It seems that I can."

WITHOUT A sustainable choice in his hand, and not able to ingest more than one vial, Khan drank the vial of ENTRANCE. The outline of a portal opened beneath them and delivered them down to a lower level about eight meters from the room. An orange spiral staircase wound its way up in front of them. It wound far up into a blank space. Each step was one meter deep and two meters long, with the following step rising to their chests. Thryn stepped onto the first step and then climbed to the second. Seconds later the first step vanished but Thryn didn't see it and continued to step onto to the third.

"Stop!" cautioned Khan.

"What?" Thryn said.

"Look!" They all saw it. "Once you leave the step it disappears. And each step has an elos character on it."

"The clues are on each step," said Griz.

"Right. It really means that if we lose the right step we can't get out. Let's just hope that it wasn't the first or second step," explained Khan.

Calwin said: "I count one hundred and twenty steps. That's one hundred and twenty choices minus the two we lost. Any one can lead to our demise. What does the locator say?"

The device was used for assistance. It also wasn't clear, but pointed upward rather than in front of them. So they moved up letting the unhappy Brak up first. He had become more quiet since his unfortunate loss of leg and masculinity though it didn't silence his bad attitude and utter disrespect for others.

Once a step was passed, it disappeared after five seconds. They moved swiftly trying to identify the right step. Each step up increased a growing pain in Calwin's head that became unbearable at the higher levels. By the ninety-ninth step, when uncertainty masked probability, they stopped. She couldn't continue under such severe pain.

"We're down to our last twenty or so," said Thryn. "Shat, if we've missed it now we'll be living on these stairs for good." He looked at the emptiness behind him that fell into an endless void.

"It may do you some good," said Griz, unexpectedly.

"What are you trying to say, helmhead?"

"Don't call me that."

"Or what?"

"Or I'll throw you into non-existence." Griz didn't even turn his face.

Thryn didn't know how to respond and ended up saying nothing.

"The locator is becoming more ambiguous. From what I read, we haven't passed the exit yet but it could be any of the next twenty-one steps," said Khan.

"Farcking great," said Brak. "This place better have some farcking treasure or I will go volatile on someone."

Khan and Griz stood on the one hundredth step; Thryn, Calwin and Brak stood on the ninety-ninth step. Calwin held her head tight, down on her haunches, with both hands to try to stop the throbbing.

"It's ironic that we are stuck on the ladder of life," said Thryn, speaking to Khan. "Moving step-by-step into who knows what. Why did I listen to you anyway?"

"I find the best adventures."

"So far, we've found nothing."

"The best is yet to come."

"The best is already gone," said Calwin, interjecting to express her loss of hope onto Khan. "The best is gone and you watched it slip away." She was reeling from the pain in her head. Thryn lent a hand to help her.

"What's wrong with you?" asked Khan.

"You! You are wrong, this place is wrong. I told you that we should have left," she said.

"We are leaving but we must find the exit—"

"The exit is on step one-hundred-and-one," she blurted out.

"What did you say?"

"The exit—" she screamed, this time in pain as her head throbbed, ready to split apart. "It's on 1-0-1!"

"How do you know?"

"One-hundred-one." Her head was tucked between her legs with both hands covering it. "Do it."

"Do it?" Khan conferred with noncommittal shoulder shrugs. "Well, let's try it."

He called out the verse inscribed on the one-hundred-and-first step and lo and behold Calwin was right. Her potion's effects had really taken shape and somehow tapped into the arvic knowledge contained nearby. An opening appeared on the right like a big serpent's mouth wanting to swallow them. One after another they jumped in and slid to the next room.

Chapter 20

THE FIVE lost and troubled party members continued to move through the subsequent rooms without any serious reaction or mistake. Khan had gained back his momentum and had learned to read the locator with precision; Calwin's sharpened arvic intellect, as a result of the potion, had increased and she pinpointed cracks in logic and answered strange riddles with seemingly little difficulty. Each room's factorial possibilities continued to expand and surmounted the odds in favor of their losing if not for the combined teamwork from the arvatist and the wind follower.

It was Thryn's aggression that became most apparent and prominent as they safely passed through from one room to the next. He despised Khan who enjoyed the glory of finding a way out for them. Calwin, his newly acquired love interest, started to lose interest in him as a capable adventurer and looked at Thryn with eyes of disappointment. Her eyes upset him the most. His jealousy of his partner and his own hidden desire to be more in charge forced him to challenge Khan's decisions more and more despite their inaccuracy. Still he continued his accusations that they were being led into the wrong direction and into Khan's own misery. Results proved different, but Thryn had a coated tongue and repetition proved a worthy opponent.

By room nine, with the party starting to consider the possibilities of the thief's accusations and no longer able to contain his views, Thryn challenged Khan's leadership.

"He's been leading us on the wrong path. I'm sure I could have found it hours ago," said Thryn.

"We're almost there—"

"You've been saying that for the last nine rooms, Khan."

"Calwin, tell Thryn over there that..."

"Khan, he's right," she said.

"He's right?" Khan said.

"Let Thryn lead."

"I agree. My leg hurts like a morbid snake bite. Let's get out of here," said Brak.

"So now it comes out, doesn't it, Calwin?"

"You've always been an absentminded leader, Khan. You overlook the greater wealth, take the most difficult path and forget the beauty of it all," said Thryn.

"He just enjoys it, the challenge of the impossible. Risk all for nothing," said Calwin. "When will you learn that life is meant for living and not for pain. Since we met, all I have seen in you is pain, Khan. You must see that."

"My only pain, stands on two legs, in front of me," replied Khan, accenting his hurt inside from what Calwin had done to him. Lutas were not providing a real comfort in his life and were distancing him further from his real expression.

"It's time to quit playing around and to stop showing off. We are here to find the tomb, in case you have forgotten," said Thryn. "You took us this far but now it's time for me to take us out."

If it hadn't been for Calwin, Khan was certain that he would have struck that two-headed thief where he was, but she was there and was the reason for his non-reaction. She was also the reason for his pain and his surrender. He opened the next portal, stood to the side, holding out the device. Thryn walked up.

"Here you are, leader," said Khan. "Lead."

"I will. This is the easy part," said Thryn.

The tenth room consisted of three spherical chambers joined together by two arched openings. The locator went crazy showing every range of color in every direction. Thryn discarded the idea of further relying on this alien device and examined his own judgment. Finally, when he was thoroughly confused as to which direction was the way out, and needing to make a decision, he called a random verse from the flooring.

The floor of the chamber lowered itself down some 100 meters into a larger spherical chamber. Once down, the platform dissolved into the invisible flat flooring. The ceiling shut and similarly vanished.

"This doesn't look good," said Brak.

"Did you know that morb decision making was not based on anything that other Seronians could understand," said Khan.

"That is why they often get killed," Griz said. He had been quiet throughout most of the last part deciding that it was best to keep his temper out of the mix unless absolutely necessary. In fact, he didn't care what happened as long as he could see Number 51. He missed her now.

Calwin's look of worry was enough to say it for all. Trouble loomed ahead. She had felt the pulse of arvicity flow through her and immediately recognized the activation of high-density arvic intentions.

CURVED WALLS started rotating in one direction but without a uniform axis of rotation. Colors and images lit up on the walls. Images of joy, sex, winning and romance. The ride became fun for a time. There was shift and the sphere spun faster and the five of them were picked up by its centrifugal force and tossed into the middle. The force became so great that eventually it seemed like the air was still in the chamber and they were floating in its stillness.

The chamber spun faster and at such a blinding speed that they soon fell unconscious except for Khan who had grown used to spinning and turbulent speeds from his wind training. As the chamber continued, bodies that touched each other began to be spliced together from the force. Two bodies were becoming one as if their very matter had been broken down into a mixture of atomic molecules once again.

It was at that time that Khan called out to Nata. He knew that she could hear him and hoped that she would come. His own wind strength was no match for the accelerator.

"Nata," he said in his head, "I need your help. I know that you can hear me and that your choice is never to be intimately involved but I have come so far and have endured so much. If this is so then there must be a reason not to end my life. Aid me, Nata, and I will serve you better. I will devote and cherish more to your learning. I cannot accept the fate of my family. It is no longer my fate!"

On the verge of he himself losing his reality equilibrium in the molecular accelerator, a path of quiet solitude emerged from his rapidity and it calmed the space that Khan was in. A couple of meters away, through a foggy blaze, stood Equist Nao; his billowing form looked directly at him for mere seconds before being torn apart into a thousand rays of colorization.

She had come, he thought, as red tears were spilled on the floor and smudged by a twist of his cora-bark adventuring boot. He tugged at his misappropriated limbs until all were once again in place and he felt whole.

Khan picked up the idle locator device. As he did, he monitored his friends. Calwin's arm touched Thryn's leg and he reached into the whirling space to push them apart. Brak and Griz had touched and their bodies began to meld together. His hands kept them separated and alive. Under the intense pressure from this ungodly machine their molecules were persuaded to bond together and in that bonding would end the life of the current being. It was like taking an entan body and splicing it into millions of tiny fragments, separating them, and fitting them together with the fragments of the rest of the bodies until the fragmented puzzle pieces of five bodies were gelled into one and then merged into the air molecules to return to the state of being nothing rather than being something. And Khan was having an increasingly difficult time keeping those body parts safely away from each other as their bodies softened into the consistency of an atomic bag.

He worked quickly, using the locator, to find a way out of this chamber. Green lit the device, an area was spotted as a possible opening, and without losing its location, he claimed Griz's clavus, and in a perilous and fatal attempt shot the clavus and himself toward the opening using the area of stale air that followed him. The weapon stuck from the force and he held onto it cracking the opening further. The weight of his body combined with the centrifugal force allowed him to rip a large chunk of the portal open, and as he was repulsed away, a strong suction immediately pulled him along with the broken chunk. The heavy battle clavus saved him from falling out the hole.

Hair and skin and clothes stretched to their limits in those sensitive fragments of halation. The hole was not big enough to save his friends so he repositioned himself and whirled around the heavy weapon. On the verge of his imminent unconsciousness stemming from lack of air, he rammed the head of the clavus into the crevasse between the chamber and an outer wall. A loud screech was heard along with the snap of the weapon's head and the room started to slow down. The four others began to reform as they quietly fell to the floor just as Khan collapsed in a heap.

"Thanks, Nata," he muttered before he too slipped into a dream.

ONE HUNDRED and 35 minutes and 41 seconds elapsed without movement nor motion. Calwin was the first to stir. She lay still as her milk returned to its proper place. Khan was still holding on to the snapped clavus shaft when he came to and used it to prop himself up. The others started to groan in their realized selves.

"What happened?" asked Calwin, still hazy from the experience.

"The obtuse leader here...made a mistake and...almost wiped us all out," said Khan, winded and hurt. His skin tingled and his limbs were still shaking uncontrollably.

"I vote for Khan to lead," said Brak, feeling like he'd just digested his own innards. All of a sudden he was happy to be alive.

"Thanks."

"Don't remember it."

"How do you know the same won't happen with me?"

"I'll take that chance," said the amputated fighter.

"So will I," said Griz. "Enough of this stupidity and seedility! I'm gonna chop the next farcking morb that takes me out the wrong portal."

"Let's get out of this first before thinking about where to go," said Khan.

The five of them, working together while ignoring Thryn, and using Calwin's arvic rope, hauled themselves out. Griz's clavus was irreparable and he refused to take Khan's only weapon in compensation. There hadn't been much use for a weapon in this complex up until this point and so Khan didn't push.

It took them three hours to find the right opening and another two hours to decipher the last puzzle: "Meddle". By then, not having the final answer, Khan was too weak from strenuous cerbal activity and had to nap before continuing. Equist Nao's face came again, shredded in a rainbow of colors as before, this time in pain. It was enough to wake him from his short sleep, and though he felt slightly revived, he also felt deep remorse and couldn't explain why.

He answered the riddle by acknowledging the importance of being a meddler, as anyone or anything who would enter this place would be called since they would be foreign. A meddler, under most circumstances would not be welcome, but this was some kind of tomb or burial or imprisonment and by its very structure and purpose combined, would make anything entering a meddler, and the only way a meddler could be accepted would be if the meddler was truly concerned with the fate and well-being of the place that was not their place by right.

He played on these terms until he could conclude that one could meddle if one was concerned. To be concerned would remove the meddle from the meddler and would make them an "r" or an "are". To be an "are" is "to be," and so, concern removed the meddler and replaced it with something that exists and can exist in this Kozotalian place of abnormality. The answer to any meddling was "concern," and with it all are given the right.

Chapter 21

WEARY ADVENTURERS, no longer meddlers, stressed
to the limit of their imagination and physically
worked beyond their masks of comfort, walked down
a hallway of statues. A carpet, engraved into the
ground matter, guided them to a portal.

They had just passed the eleventh portal and all
signs on the locator glowed green. It was the last.
All of them walked with a greater sense of self, that
they had reached limits, inherent in entans and
karul, and were thankful of being alive. Only two of
them, Khan and Griz, moved with a subliminal
difference: as if mortality lived further from their
essences, as if they could not die unless they chose
to. Khan and Griz were less happy to be alive than

they were to know the taste of immortality and its possibilities.

Each translucent statue, five on each side and half a meter taller than Griz, was molded by flamma and held their own unique color. Kozotalian heroes by Calwin's estimation. The workmanship was perfect in every way, a magnificence of the masters of creation. Double doors, tall and of the same craftsmanship, waited at the end of this majestic hallway.

As they reached the center of the hallway, the statues opened their eyes – the five of them jerked into defensive positions – and wide rays of flamma engulfed them all but it was not flamma that burned them—no, the flamma revived and cleansed them of their stresses. They calmed and stayed to bathe in the light.

The doors opened automatically into a large chamber. The inside was shaped like a pyramid, flattened on its side with the wider end at the back, but instead of a flat wall it was concave, curved inwards and gently pointing its round edge at the doors they stood at. The highest point in the ceiling, according to Calwin's estimate, was 9 meters, the widest point in the chamber was 99 meters.

Glass walls etched and engraved in every space and continuum of colorful trees, transparent beings, and vivid rainbows cast out of palms only to be swallowed by hollow mouths; and, most impressive, two dancing Seragons playing with a round ball of white flamma that did not scorch them.

In front of the curvature was a large spherical mist, dense in opacity, and approximately 4.5 meters in diameter. It held a dull glow.

To the right side of the chamber was a giant throne, cast of the same glassy material, beside the throne were two statues of half-Kozotal and half-Seragon beasts three meters in height. They each held a staff in one hand. Directly opposite the throne at the wall was a beautifully carved glass statue of a Kozotal.

To their immediate left and right, as they entered into the chamber, were two areas staged with goods. Guarding the double doors were two statues with long open hands held in front, palms facing in, of their massive chests. On the left of the doors were chests of treasure and hand-carved items that sparkled of value. To their right was a rack of weapons including several flat-bladed batiers, a clavus, and miscellaneous objects including a gleaming black helm that reflected the flamma emitted in this room.

KHAN NOTICED it first. The entire chamber had no temperature. No wind or breeze. Fresh air. Sound did not travel far. All was mysteriously lit and immaculately clean. And all was quiet except for the hum coming from the large misty ball.

"This is it," Khan said. "Be careful so that we may understand such mysteriousness."

"Who's been paying the maid?" said Thryn.

"Farck the maid!" added Brak. "And grant me a farcking seat. I tire in our trek to the tomb. This is not a tomb like any I have seen—How about a hand?"

Brak had been pushing his strength for hours. The signs of weariness were very evident in his voice – because of his rude personality it was difficult to distinguish the difference – and had softened him as of late. Khan helped Brak to the throne and set him down.

"You get the best seat. Just don't let it go to your head," Khan said.

"Listen, Khan. I'm sorry," said Brak.

"Sorry about what?"

"About what happened before."

"Don't concern yourself with it. Let's just get our dues and get out." Khan left to inspect another area.

"My leg is killing me!—Everybody, I deserve more treasure." Brak's rationality couldn't last long.

"You'll get the same as all of us," Thryn said.

"Like a morb is going to suck my butt, I will. Look at my leg!" Brak yelled. "And I can't feel my penis any—"

"You should be more careful."

"Come here, you farck. I'll pop your head like a sack of mud!"

"Keep quiet you fat morb. You might just scare something up." Thryn looked around for secret hiding places that special treasure might lay.

"Thryn, shut the farck up!" Calwin said.

"Thryn, have a look around. Everyone on alert including you, Brak," said Khan. "Griz, get ready."

"My spell casting is weakening," said Calwin, worry in her voice. "There is no river here."

"What are you saying?" said Thryn.

"Spells only work with arvicity and in this chamber there is no arvicity. And there is no river of arvicity in which I can tap into to recharge my stores. As my stores are used up we will have no more spells for I have no place to acquire new arvic energy."

"Reserve your stores," said Khan. "We don't want to make haste in here, not until we understand what the environment really is."

"Excuse me, Khan," Thryn started, perturbed by the incessant caution by his thieving partner, "but this is not an archeological exploration in which we are trying to record some historical morbshat. We're thieves!—Remember? Farck the understanding shat and let's get to the farcking treasure."

A drum sounded, one deep beat, that none heard.

"Do you always want to have sex with your pants on?"

"What does sex have to do with—"

"Everything! Everything. This environment, this place can seriously hurt us. It is amazing that we are alive. Before you start jumping into bed you should pull off your pants or it's going to be very messy."

The eyes of the two statues by the double doors lit up. Khan spotted them.

"Be ready! By the door!" cried Khan. The two statues, each over three meters high, stepped down from their short pedestal. They gleamed of silvery glass. One marched directly toward Thryn, the other for Calwin.

"What—" said Thryn, turning to see two statues come to life.

"Watch out!" Brak said.

"Calwin!" Khan yelled.

Calwin screamed as the statue waded through the table between it and her. It cornered her. As it approached it reached out an open palm and Calwin could feel herself slowing down as if the very space she inhabited had become smaller and she could no longer move. The second palm came out and reached for the top of her head. Khan ran over but was knocked back by an invisible shield surrounding them. She could not move at all by then and was left vulnerable to the hand that touched her. Griz came over and his fists bounced off as fast and hard as they came.

"Calwin! Get out of the way!"

It was then that her body, kol and all was dematerialized into atomic matter and rematerialized inside of the statue. Once complete, the statue stopped and became semi-transparent.

The second statue caught Thryn with the same result. The other three could not understand what was going on nor could they pierce the shield that encircled the two of them.

"What's happening to them?" asked Griz.

"I could not begin to guess," said Khan. "This place is strange for a tomb. I am beginning to imagine that it is not a tomb in the traditional sense, if at all. It is like a closet." Griz didn't understand.

"A closet is used for storage whereas a tomb is for burial. There is a difference, you know."

"No, I do not know of such things."

"I guess you haven't been to many burials."

"I just like to kill the enemy. I leave the mess to others."

"This place is looking more and more like a place of storage than of burial. And we are the foreign guests." Khan went on. "Tombs are usually, and I use the term loosely, sealed to preserve the life and sanctity of the dead; be it a statue or not. Escarotian's Tomb is unique because of a couple of reasons I can think of: For one, it is an island on the end of a sea of mazes that only certain kinds of beings – crazy ones like us – could safely navigate. This suggests to me that the tomb desperately does not want to be found or that it could not be contained on Seranor.

"For two, the environment is complex but not hostile. It is as if the tomb is a place of storage rather than burial. It may also assimilate and process before storage."

"They shouldn't sell it as a farcking tomb if it's a closet," Griz said, unhappy to hear the news after entering this place.

GRIZ, BORED by the lack of anything to strike and without any cold anaprimo, hit the weapons area examining the black helm. He considered it unnecessary in here and picked up the clavus instead. It was a well-balanced gray, two-handed and made of a lutium mix. Satisfactory. What was distinctive was the sharp blade. To his recollection, the blade of a clavus had never been sharp but dull so that it could break porcelan more easily thereby subduing the opponent. This weapon was made to cut and to kill. He took an immediate liking to his new clavus.

To his left he noticed a thick chain, a warrior's girdle, black on black of unscratched material, finished together in a thick buckle fastened at the center. Instantly impressed by it, he put down the clavus and put on the girdle. It reenergized him with renewed strength and an effervescence appeared in his eyes that no other saw.

"I see that you are spending great effort on solving the predicament at hand," Khan said to his new brother.

"They look okay," Griz said.

"What the farck is happening to them? Does anyone know?" said Brak, he had temporarily fallen asleep in the comfort of the throne chair.

"It doesn't seem to be hurting them in any way. That is a good sign. I would even guess that it is helping them."

"How can those glass statues be helping them in this morbfarcking tomb? Can you tell me that? This is the place of the dead. At the very least, all of these statues in here are designed to wipe our butts as quickly as they came in. That's how tombs are built."

"Maybe it's not a tomb," said Khan.

"Then what is it? A recreation center?" Brak was frustrated.

"It's a closet," interjected Griz.

"A what?"

"Stop and use your cerbus for a minute," said Khan. "Look, if it was a tomb then there would be far more resistance against us. We would encounter spells, death traps and killer statues until we were extinguished or were out of here. But this place offers no such hostile environment. In fact, it is very safe for a tomb."

"It is the tomb of a Kozotal so maybe it's special in how it kills us."

"Maybe, but Kozotal are beings of creation not destruction. To have them kill us with contradict their making."

"Some of those rooms almost killed us."

"I don't know if you could say that they tried to kill us as much as you could say that those rooms were made for the non-Kozotal. In other words, only the Kozotal could be capable of walking to the right rooms."

"Them and Nivians."

"What did you say?"

"Them and Nivians."

"Nivians?" Khan felt for the locator device. He asked himself, could a Nivian have made such a device to navigate the realm of the Kozotal? He didn't know. His fingers rubbed the fine casting of the object.

"Khan! Look!" yelled Brak from the seat.

The once invisible shield surrounding Calwin and Thryn turned yellow. The two bodies inside radiated more health than before.

"We are useless like this," said Khan. "I wish to do something but what that is I do not know. None of us use arvicity. We are forced to watch and to wait."

CALWIN'S STATUE was the first to start moving. As it did the yellowed spherical shield around it cracked into a pile of dust on the floor and her body rematerialized from the outstretched palm. Thryn followed seconds later.

Khan was there for comfort. "Calwin, are you okay? Can you hear me? Are you hurt in some way? Please say something to soothe my cerbind."

"I'm okay."

"What happened?"

"I was taken away to an ugly place and…"

"And what?" he looked at her then at Thryn for some answers.

"…and in this ugly place I found myself facing you."

"Me?"

"Yes. You were there taking me up a dark mountain and into the hands of a blackened being emitting massive amounts of arvicity. I know that it was arvicity because of the way that it burned my skin. But you would not stop and forced me to touch this powerful being until I was a melted pile of ceramic flesh. You would not stop and I could not resist. And then something strange occurred."

"What?"

"It was very strange because of how it happened."

"What is it, Calwin?"

"I was sitting there as a pile of clay and then I was reformed into me – just as I am now – and then I was allowed to leave the mountain and return to a peaceful place full of luxurious wants."

"And me? What happened to me, Calwin? What happened to me?"

"You—You remained on the mountain until you vanished."

"That's not good."

"But it does suit your character, does it not?— Anyway, I feel better now than I have felt in tios. As if I am purified from my emotions."

"I too feel cleansed but mine was a most painful one," said Thryn. "I feel that I had nearly died in there."

"I am glad that you did not die, Thryn," said Calwin. She moved up close to him and hugged him tight. He hugged back.

Khan angrily watched on. Griz looked at him suggesting him to disrupt their embrace but Khan knew that their relationship had ended and was happy to have it finish, finally.

He was getting proficient at finding and losing relationships like earning and spending zorn after a successful adventure. This process of accumulation and redistribution was imbibing him with a need, a need to go on and to continue the process. It was an interaction that strengthened him, not for loving one, but for loving more than one. This process expanded his ability to love others and it made him consider – at the back of his cerbind – whether or not this love process was making him more distant to his own love and to who he was and what he was for. This question probed him: What am I made for? The emotional high provided by continuous short-term relationships was just that: a temporary stimulation. A distraction for his corius so that he would not need to understand any further about himself.

Eventually, he thought, this process would require a kind of alteration. Eventuality would come. He was more sure of that than finding a way out of this false tomb alive.

Chapter 22

CALWIN RECOMPOSED herself and studied the nearest statue. "Only a powerful arvician could create these—"

"Or an arvicerer," said Khan. "Escarotian was a Kozotal with unknown power at his disposal. These statues—"

"Were not real statues. They were cleansers of sorts."

"To clean what?"

"To clean the things that entered here."

"That is to mean us."

"In this case, yes."

"I think that she is right," said Thryn.

"Why is that so easy to understand?" asked Khan sarcastically.

"Stop it," Calwin said.

"When I was caught inside the statue I did not feel in danger of the statue. I did feel though in danger of myself," Thryn explained.

"I was surprised that they did not attack us," said Khan. "I originally feared they were only a distraction to facilitate some other action."

"It tried to remove something from me. Something painful like a short batier piercing my neck." Khan imagined that scene and smiled as the thief spoke. "And in its removal there was the risk of death, not physical, but emotional. It is odd that I can even speak about this now since I have never considered much about em0tion and now it is all I am beginning to consider."

"Why the two of you?"

"Who knows."

The two statues had not moved from their last position and had become yellowish in color. The yellow deepened as the minutes passed.

"In any case, I don't think we should stay here long," she said.

"What guards this place from raiders is a cleanser," Thryn said to no one in particular. "How do you resist against that?"

Brak, frustrated by his inability to participate, stomped Octo's head several times beside the throne chair and then hurled the weighted shaft at the ball of mist.

"I'll look for a way out," she said.

"Good idea, Cal—" added Thryn, ignoring his friend's misbehavior.

"Cal, is it?" said Khan. Thryn shrugged his shoulders.

"So tell us, Khan. Where is the defense mechanism of the great flamma gods?"

"Probably where you have just been."

"What does that mean?"

"This place was inhabited by a creator of life. It does not attack you with traps or weapons. These are tools for seedlings—"

"Then what?"

"It is hard to imagine...

"Take a guess."

"A cleanser is a good start."

"There has got to be more than that."

"If I were to guess," Khan said, "I would say that it has already begun to influence us but we cannot see it. It may even by a sound imperceptible to our entan hearing. The sound of death and the end of our illustrious fuse..."

Thryn was being drowned in philosophy and tried to stay in the conversation: "If it's imperceptible, how would we hear it?" he asked and then realized his very stupid question to which Khan just turned away before moving closer to inspect the statue opposite the throne chair.

The cloudy glass fiber used to make this lone statue was indeed different. Khan sensed the material with his fingers. Not a dimple or a rough edge anywhere. Not only that but the details were much like exact replication of real life save the fact that the statue wore minimal clothing, a loose fitted rainbow skirt tied at the waist by a yellow sash. All the colors were washed out and partially see-through. A handsome body fitted the face and an ounce of pain was detected in its wry smile.

A STREAM of mist lashed out from the whitish sphere and hit Brak encompassing his entire body and cerbind. A handsome Brak walked in a cora field with a single-handed hammer in his hand. He approached a young voluptuous luta, beat her several times, raped her and then murdered her with the blunt hammer. He grinned the whole time, felt the excitement in his murderous glory. A small valuable necklace was taken and sold for much less than its worth; he bought himself a room at an inn and had copious amounts of sex with a senseless karuli prostitute. She slapped him repeatedly during the time he entered her all the while with a serious tone in her voice. It took a good three slaps to wipe the hazy eyes from Brak. Thryn actually enjoyed that part. Brak's grin lasted a little longer.

"You farck! What are you doing?" asked Thryn.

"Nothing. I must have been dreaming. Why?" said Brak.

"Do you always grin when you dream?"

"I can't see if I'm sleeping, now can I?"

"A shot of mist came out and hit you."

"Really? I didn't see anything."

"Yes, really. Each minute that passes makes you more of a farcking moron."

"Farck you."

Thryn returned to his claiming of treasure; Griz enjoyed his new strength; Calwin studied the arvicity in the chamber; and Khan searched for a way out after picking up a new batier and finding a little purple sack that could hold much more than its external size indicated. He quickly filled it with some jewelry just to give it some weight then dumped it for a larger block of a carved white Kozotal that sparkled with zorn in his eyes. This filled the sack to a point near its limit.

The humming drum from when they first entered had incrementally grown in loudness but they hadn't noticed because it raised up pitch-by-pitch, decibel-by-decibel. The sound soon drowned them in their dreams and all cerbinds floated away in its rhythm.

Griz saw an old luto making strange potions in his residence. He himself was heavily armored carrying a double-bladed two-handed clavus. He approached the luto, unable to surprise him and was recognized very clearly; and hacked repeatedly until nothing but small pieces of what was once entan remained. A single red tear dropped into the pool of milk on the floor splashing a tainted pink goop all over him.

The armored warrior cleared from his dream state and continued to check over the weapons.

A spot of pinkish milk lay on the table.

There in the place where Calwin and Khan first met from his episode with Boon the thief, Calwin found herself once again. The stranger, Shev'la, came inside asking for zorn and instead of turning to face him, she ran away never to be seen again.

Shev'la held her milky corius, still beating, in his hands and he cried.

Calwin found herself with her hand on the wall as she had been just doing. As she moved her hand, it uncovered an engraving of a Seragon's corius.

Thryn could not help to remember the familiar place where Khan was kept after being taken in by Captain T. Rain. While in jail, Thryn was allowed in with two short batiers and without sound or speech stabbed Khan twice through the head and chest. He died there in his jail cell with Thryn laughing.

The banging of valuable carvings and jewelry returned him to his modern vision. Thryn was laughing loudly. None of the others were staring but he still felt embarrassed.

Khan raced up an ice mountain, dead set on his mission to kill Zorath. A black bodied figure stepped out and the two battled fiercely but Khan's weapon was no match for the Nivian King. Khan's head was removed and his statuesque body tossed off the mountain, tumbling down into the blackness.

The wind follower woke and found himself on the ground after having tripped over an unseen table. His head hit a goblet hard denting the surface and warping his reflection. It reminded him of his father and his ream of optimism and encouragement for possibilities, flawed at best. The foundation of life slept in a world of would could be.

Chapter 23

A BLOCK of elos was engraved on the far end of the chamber near the left wing. Calwin couldn't understand it.

"Khan, there's something here," she said.

The writing told the story of a planetary reawakening by an elemental reunification. Khan read part of it: ELEMENTS JOIN IN PASSION'S LOIN/ MOTHER REBORN IN COLD SCORN. He translated as best he could. "There is more here, but it is an ancient elos. Doesn't make sense."

While Khan read on, Calwin and Thryn sifted through the treasure. They uncovered many ceremonial items made of valuable materials, as well as a white ring, a wide bracelet, and the gleaming black helm. It was a full helm, finely crafted lutium with a wide black face.

"The helm's mine!" yelled Brak. Thryn threw it to his old friend; he had no interest in such idiotic pieces of equipment.

"No, it's not." Griz said, moving up to grab one end of it.

"It's mine."

"Actually, I found it first. And I lost my helm before we entered the lake." Griz lifted him out of the throne chair, one leg and all, with one arm. His strength far surpassed any other Seronian thanks to the girdle.

"Farck, you're strong! I lost a leg for it, you didn't. A leg is more valuable than a helm. You can buy a new helm but it will take me a long time to buy a new leg." He looked at Brak's missing lower leg, grunted once and let him go. Brak dropped down hard, too happy to notice the bruises.

"Consider it a favor," said Griz.

"Calwin, check this out for me." She cast a spell on the helm.

"It is a helm of...its not clear...of vision and breath. It will allow you to breath in any environment,"

"Just what I need."

"There's something inconsistent about it. I don't know if it's the chamber or the helm."

"It must be the chamber."

"Do not be so sure, Brak. It is true about the lack of arvicity here. I do not doubt that. There is also something about this helm."

"What does that mean?" He prepared to place it on his head.

"Wait!" said Khan. "What is the rush? We'll have time later. Let's just get out of here, first."

"Do you see my leg?"

"No," replied Thryn.

"Of course not, it was chopped off. At least this is compensation for losing my leg." He hastily placed it on and the room became very clear and his breathing improved. He felt more alive. "This thing is incredible. I feel great!" Brak looked around then up and down excited at his new toy.

Just then, the entire helm went transparent and sealed itself off at the neck.

"Get it off! Get it off!" He screamed. "I can't breathe!"

"Calwin, can you dispel it?" Khan asked, hoping for a "yes."

She was already there casting a spell and shaking her head. "It's too high for me."

"Get it off! Help!" Brak screamed, his eyes bulging. Khan worked his hands, even punched it trying to remove it, without success. The bottom of the helm flashed brightly and closed itself off on all sides until it hit the neck bone. Brak's head dropped limp to the back. He died instantly, falling on Khan's chest with a helm full of his own milk.

"Stupid moron," said Khan. "Can an entan be more stupid than this idiot? All you had to do was listen. That's with a capital 'L'. Was that so hard?"

The body slid off and crashed onto the floor.

"Who would do this?" asked Thryn, angry that he lost his annoying friend.

"An arvicerer with malicious intent," Calwin said.

"Not a Kozotal's work. Must be a lot of things from outside here. Be careful. We don't know what power or destiny lies in some of this stuff."

Khan gave Griz a look that said he was lucky he let Brak take it.

"Well, he was a pain in the ass anyway," said Thryn, changing the mood. "That luto could make aqua embarrassed if he tried. Shat, he's just one less to pay."

Griz was lucky to be alive and he knew it.

"Nice girdle, Griz. That's going to be counted as treasure," said Khan. The armored warrior didn't seem to care at all. He walked over to one of the large tables, lifted it and threw it a good ten meters. "That girdle suits your character just fine," said Khan smiling. "Must be a girdle of strength."

"What did you take?" asked Griz.

"So far?"

"Yes."

"So far, just this small sack of holding." He held the purple sack, no bigger than his hand but inside he pulled out the item just to show Griz its capabilities.

"Cute. Useless, but cute."

"Kind of like lutas, huh," added Thryn while Calwin was preoccupied.

"I heard that," she said.

Chapter 24

MUCH HAD happened in only a short time. It was
the rule of adventure on Seranor that life positively
changed; and not necessarily changed positively.
Some were fortunate, others drowned in their own
dreams. No one knew why or how dreams
materialized for one and dematerialized for others
though some believed that it was all connected to the
will of the Versos and the cosmic struggle that all
life within Aquanomicus would continue. And for it
to continue, life must equivocally have death and
demise. Balance was only maintained from the
dichotomy of two extremes. An elegant interaction.
It was the dance of opus and ora. It was the will of
the cosmos.

Thryn immediately lost his feelings for his dead friend and replaced it with two items he now held in his hands – a ring and a bracelet. They were not of a set and definitely embedded with arvic intentions.

"Calwin, what does this ring and bracelet do?" he asked.

A white mist from Calwin's hand hugged the items. "This ring prevents the severing of limbs and it automatically rejoins a severed limb once reattached, but this power drains the ring for months." She put the ring down and picked up the bracelet.

"We should have found this a half-day ago," said Thryn, laughing.

"The bracelet is an arvic shield," Calwin started. "All who wear it will be protected from arvicity. I do not know how much or how long it will protect you. You must touch it with the other hand in order to activate its power. I will keep this, I think."

"I want you to keep this, my dear Calwin."

"Thank you, Thryn."

"Are the two of you going to need some time alone?" said the bitter Khan.

Spending more time in the chamber caused them to dream again, this time, they fought each other in their dreams, and by the third dream, all were dead.

Time was short, they had to get out. Khan found a possible exit at a single door on the far right wing. It led down a hallway into an unlocked portal. Behind the portal was a black impenetrable mist.

"Khan!" Calwin screamed, worried about Khan and his curiosity, calling him back to the chamber.

He had reached the halfway point between him and the mist when a smoky black being floated out. "Danger!" Khan screamed. He dashed away after his batier cut through thin air but the blackness engulfed him and stole him into the room he had just opened, before his third step. He was gone. No trace of him existed except for the locator spinning on the ground.

Thryn nabbed Calwin and they frantically searched for an exit. Griz stood in front of the large ball.

On the other side of the chamber, in the left wing, was another single door made of radiolucent glass. She used the locator's crystal to find its command and two of them entered a curved hallway. Griz arrived at the archway and waited.

The hallway curved around until it touched the wall that sat behind the large sphere of mist. One elos character was inscribed and translated to a close interpretation of EXIT. Calwin pulled herself away from Thryn's grip and ran to fetch Griz. His eyes gave it away first and were what stopped her legs from continuing on.

"Griz, we're leaving," said Calwin.

"I will find Khan first," he replied.

"If you stay you will die in here."

"Maybe I will die out there. Death is certain. I will find Khan and we will leave together."

"If he wants to stay then let him. We've got enough treasure for the two of us. We're rich, Calwin. Come on," said Thryn, trying to persuade her.

"Listen, Griz. Don't follow him. He's insane and you will end up dead sooner rather than later," said Calwin.

"Go before it is too late." Griz headed towards the right wing where he would find the black mist.

Weakened beyond exhaustion, Calwin, nearly drained of her arvicity, and Thryn; escaped with enough wealth to propel each other into real luxury.

Chapter 25

UNKNOWN TIME elapsed as the two adventurers wrestled with their mysterious black immaterial forms.

As they moved further and further away from reality, the blackness spread out and grew into a fog that filled every crevice of a large, otherwise empty space without borders; each of them wandered around aimlessly with the intention to keep moving as a sign of living. It was a dense fog with a source of crispy colored light shining from some unidentifiable location centralized over one region and was what attracted the two of them to find each other.

"Khan," said Griz, happy to see his friend alive. "You live."

"For the moment," Khan replied. "Where are the others?"

"Calwin and Thryn have left," said Griz, groggy from the excursion. He was still recovering from the disorientation and regaining his composure and bearings.

"Then why didn't you go with them?" Khan asked, hoping that he would be left alone to wallow in his joylessness.

"Party members stay together. You taught me that," Griz said.

"You are sure not what a lot of Seronians thought you'd be."

"Neither are you." It was Griz's attempt at a smart remark that made Khan fall into an uncontrollable laugh. The remark was a final push over the high edge that he had endured since back in Casus and the episodes with Calwin. Now, after expending massive amounts of cerbal energy to get his party out safe all was lost, all that he loved was thrown to the beach, left for fodder in the wind. The laugh made all the icy hurt melt into flowing aqua and he bathed in its love. His friend followed in his own deep burst of joviality.

Khan and Griz searched for the source of colored light hoping that it would help them, hoping that it was the right choice in this otherwise deathly existence.

Griz occasionally saw images of his father, a old hurt billowed inside his corius spewing forth the memories he once chose to forget. Khan was haunted by his family. The family that left him alone on the planet. And it had been after Anativo was discovered that all real pain began; alone like he was now, if not for Griz's presence.

They rested many times, some periods just faded away in a mysterious place, but each time they came back to search for a way out. Time in this place was affecting them; their skin was graying much like the fog.

"We must find a way out, Griz. Our time has lost its luxury," said the wind follower.

"This luxury that you speak of only keeps memories, memories that I do not want."

They continued their search for the source of light entering a clearing where the fog separated and left a circular opening. All sides including the floor was made of the same dark material.

"What is this place?" asked Griz.

"I am not certain. But there is activity here. If there is activity, there is life. Be careful."

The two cautiously stepped inside.

Moments later, a beautiful Kozotal female wearing light and yellow-colored cora silks walked up to greet them. "Welcome, Shev'la Khan and Roman Griz-Rymthoran. I am Tyla, your guide here."

"Where are we and how do you know our names?" asked Khan.

"You are neither here nor there. Names, names are meant to be known when needed just as we have shared," she said. "Why have a name if it cannot be remembered?"

"How do we get out?"

"Only I know the way out."

"And will you tell us?" asked Griz, sarcastically.

"Ever since your speech has improved, you have grown somewhat cynical, Griz. Did you know that we don't become anything new, we only express what we have always been?"

"You haven't answered my friend's question, Tyla," said Khan.

"If you want to know the way out, you must assist me with three problems."

"You've got problems?" They had no choice but to play her game for the time being.

"I'm not finished," she said. "Fail to solve them correctly and I will no longer help you and you will be trapped here forever. That translates into a long long time. Perform correctly and you will be free. But each problem solved must have valid reasoning to justify it."

Khan looked at Griz. "It's our best choice for now. Let's try it."

"Not your best choice, Khan. Your only choice in this place," said Tyla.

"Listen luta, don't get me noxied up or you won't like it," said Griz, raising a clenched fist. Not a single response of fear was evident.

"First, tell us who you are?" asked Khan.

"I am Tyla."

"Where are we, Tyla?"

"Where all things come from. The well of creation."

"Where exactly is that?" asked Griz. "It's not Casus."

"Forget the location for it means nothing if you do not pass this game. You might as well have been nothing than what you are if you don't pass. Are you ready to play?"

Khan looked at Griz. They agreed. "Alright. We will assist you," Khan said.

"Remember, fail to solve and consider your lives finished."

"Open and ask."

"We begin with the first problem: Is an equal amount of kium to cora stronger?"

Khan had the answer to this. "No."

She hesitated at first. "Are you certain of this answer?"

"Yes," he replied.

"You may confirm with your friend if you wish. I will allow you that."

"That is not necessary. I will keep my answer." Griz didn't know anyway.

"Fine. Tell me why?"

"Cora folded hundreds of times, pressed and wet with anaprimo can break kium."

"Good. It is correct. You have completed the first. Onto the next: Which can penetrate more deeply, love or flamma."

Griz bumped Khan's shoulder. "I'll answer this one. It is love."

"Is it?"

"Yes. Love can penetrate the entire planet. I know this because my lack of it hurts me no matter where I am."

"That is acceptable, brutal warrior. In a fight, Griz, could you kill your father?"

"Yes," Griz answered.

"Are you certain?"

"Yes."

"Then you have not only failed the last problem but also lied to yourself."

"That wasn't even a question. You tricked me."

"No tricks. You have lied, Griz."

"Griz, is that true?" asked Khan.

"She lies!" Griz moved up. "Listen you—"

"Careful with your anger, liar. Temper can kill love."

"Griz, maybe it's not a good idea."

"This luta is the real liar."

"No. Stop!" cried Khan, locking his friend's arm who then turned on him.

FROM GRIZ'S view he only saw the face and figure of his father. Tyla watched on, a cunning smile on her lush lips. The first fist missed. The second hit Khan's shoulder nearly separating it from its socket. "Stop!" Griz wouldn't listen. His temper had got the best of him and an entire youth of unexpressed emotion came out in raw form against his only friend. Khan saw that something was wrong and despite repeated calls to stop he knew that he had to fight him or he would die. Griz came on strong and Khan used his refined movements, his own wind effects were subdued because of the environment, to wear down his opponent. There was no way to stop him without seriously hurting him.

It was after he called out "father!" twice that he put together the problem and then changed his approach to try to reach Griz as his father might. He grabbed the armored warrior and locked him in a tight grapple, known to Equists as the wind's cuff.

"Roman Griz-Rymthoran, I am sorry for what I have done to you," said Khan, acting like a would-be father.

"You are not sorry! You have deformed me! You have taken!" Griz cried.

"I am sorry for what I have done. Please forgive me. Forgive me!"

"No! You killed mother and you sent me away. Why did you send me away? Why?" Griz eyes reddened with tears.

"It was a mistake. A mistake!"

Griz's unnatural strength could not be contained even by the wind's cuff and Khan went flying into the mist, hurt and broken.

"Father! Father! Why?! Why did you hurt me?" cried Griz as he landed on his knees crying for the love that he had been denied his whole life.

Khan, breathing hard over his injuries, called out and said: "Griz, it is the female who tricks us now. Tyla, she is now taking from you. Will you also let her take?"

"Khan?—Female!" he yelled. "Tyla will die!" He charged, surprised her as her legs went out and she fell hard on her back with Griz on top.

She remained calm. "Kill me and you will never leave."

"Farck you!" The fists came fast and furious pounding her into the ground. As soon as the second fist crunched in her head, her body disappeared and Griz's illusion went away with it.

"Is she gone?" Khan asked looking for a signal of safety. Milk dripped from some wounds.

This time Griz knew his friend's voice. "She is gone," he said, wiping his face of tears and stopping his crying.

"Are you okay?" Khan returned, semi-worn over the battle.

"Yeah. Griz thinks so."

"But we are still in this place," said Khan, disappointed at his realization.

"What was she?" asked his strong friend.

Khan said: "A manifestation, I mean, an image that was trying to weaken us, trying to trap us by casting fear in what hurts us the most. Believe what she tells us and we would never leave. An illusion like the real. This place is some kind of realm of the subconscious."

"Farck fear," said Griz. "The only thing to fear is my gauntlet when my fist is in it."

"If it can do that, keep it handy, friend."

"I am sorry that I hit you."

"I was looking for some exercise. Just don't make a habit of it. Shat, you nearly took my head off a couple of times," said the wind warrior.

"Good thing you've kept up your training," replied the unhelmed Griz.

"What happened between your father and you?"

"He distorted my body, my cerbind, then discarded me after he killed my mother. I am what I am because of his influence and after he had inflicted his wounds he cast me out. He no longer wanted me. I have lost my family by my father's hand."

"It is this notion of family that we have in common, Griz."

"Why?"

"My entire family was slaughtered. They are all dead. They have abandoned me as has Calwin, and if not for you, I cannot think of where I would be."

"Then let us remember this day," said Griz.

"Let's rest up and then try to get ourselves out of this mess," replied Khan.

"No need to lock my wrist for that. The thief has got some dues still unpaid."

The gray mist surrounded the two worn travelers trying to obscure their presence, and if not for the movement of mist as they walked through it, there would cease to exist any form of life in Escarotian's Tomb. Khan and Griz moved carefully and with each step the mist grew a darker shade and their bodies weakened as they searched for a way out.

Chapter 26

THE TWO trapped adventurers deduced that keeping
the search for the source of brightly colored light was
the best option as everything else around them was
dark fog and there was a warmth coming from the
presence of flamma. Khan and Griz wandered
around trying to find its source. The flamma glowed
from all directions as if without source and it was
this fact that made it difficult to find. Griz had an
idea.

"Khan, the flamma is all around us but does not
pass over us."

"Interesting," replied Khan.

"Can you create some wind and blow this fog
away?"

"Funny, I didn't think of that." Khan prepared his wind stance. "Griz, keep a watchful eye as I remove this fog." He breathed deeply, then called Nata. Nothing. She was not to be heard.

"I am waiting."

"She's not here."

"Who?"

"Nata."

"Who?"

"There is no wind here. I cannot call it."

"Why?"

"I need wind."

"Try without it."

"It's not possible."

"Try, Khan. As you taught me that speaking will improve my language then trying will summon your wind."

"Using my own words against me. Okay."

"You are the wind."

"I am the wind."

He took his wind stance again. This time he did not call Nata but called inside to his own influential space and seeing something held it, squeezed hard and released it. His body swirled and Khan as the wind spun the fog away. Even Griz was taken off his feet to a short distance from where he stood.

Griz looked around and saw a bright white spot far to their left about five or six meters from the ground. He ran over as Khan continued his windy stir. Then as Griz was reaching it the wind died down, the wind form lost its effects. He ran faster to catch it and managed to stand under it just before the black fog returned.

Khan hopped onto Griz's hands and he was thrown up. He caught a glowing multi-colored cylinder that, when removed from its stillness, stopped lighting the room and only lit a small radius around the holder. The fog outside of their lit area had become pitch black.

"Here is our flamma." He tossed Khan the fat object. It was cylindrical in shape, exactly 13 centimeters across and 18 centimeters high. Upon it was carved beautiful drawings in full color both above and below the central, deeply-engraved piece containing intertwined serpents. At the bottom, wrapped around the entire cylinder, were eighteen ancient elos characters. It was of an unknown material, without openings, locks, or anything distinguishable to a Seronian eye. The colorful flamma it emitted was warm and soothing. And its weight shifted from heavy to light as an oblong ball rolled down a hill. Because it stood in one place the shifting weight felt like a throbbing.

"These first three characters represent its name," said Khan.

"What does it say?" asked Griz.

"It is called, Pyxacognitartis."

"What does it mean?"

"These characters can have several meanings. Probably means something like 'the box of thinking art' or the 'art of a thinking box' or 'art is thought in a box'." Khan looked it over carefully trying to decipher the other characters.

"It is still bright," said Griz.

"Yes," said Khan. He noticed that the flamma pierced the small radius of the black fog. "*This* will get us out of here."

The wind maker also saw that their bodies were become whole once more in the presence of this box.

"How did it come to be here?"

"That I cannot answer. It is as if we are in Escarotian's cerbind and we have found the storehouse of his intellect. What remains of it, anyway."

"Is that where we are, Khan, his cerbind?"

"Maybe it is his subconscious – the cockpit – and we have become ideas in their early formation," Khan said, laughing. "We are messages after all. My father showed me that." He held the cylinder up as it shined the ceramic highlights of their faces. "We are data on a mission who have found a way out of our desperation. Thanks to our cooperation."

THEY WALKED around with the lit cylinder until they eventually found a hole where gusts of blackness were sucked in and out in rapid succession. Using Khan's windy stance for safety, they forced their way through the hole and back into the chamber.

Brak's body was gone along with all the other contents except for the humming misty ball which had doubled in size and continued to expand. Only the glass-like encasing remained and it too was warping, ready to snap at any second.

Khan exchanged the statue in his purple sack for the flamma object, Pyxacognitartis. They raced to the exit, their footsteps drowned by the loud hum. Just as he called out the verse, the walls snapped under intense pressure and the entire chamber was being swallowed into the spherical mist. Khan's hand reached out to Griz and pulled him inside.

They reappeared in the rough corridor they had entered and picked up the discarded locator on the ground. The damp walls were replaced with dried rock. Walking slowly, mostly from a lethargic body that had gone without food and aqua, they reached the underaqua exit. The gate was open and also dry. The lake was gone including all of its contents. Only an open chasm where a lake once existed was left. Astonished but driven to leave, they started climbing.

When they reached the top they saw that the shore was only hundreds of meters away, not the many kilometers they had traveled when they first arrived.

Khan and Griz were puzzled at what had happened. They drank plenty of aqua to replenish their bodies and noticed that the island was still sinking at a rapid rate. Khan estimated a day at most.

Ten hours later the two of them finished building a functional boat from the tree trunks and leaves. Griz's immense strength was matched with Khan's creativity. They started off in their makeshift boat watching the island drown in the ocean.

ONCE A safe distance away, Khan examined the glowing object more closely. He decided to keep PYXACOGNITARTIS and grew attached to it during their journey back to Casus. He would also put it out of plain sight, just in case there were questions raised about it, and hid it in his purple sack of holding.

Just as the pleasure of survival left their cerbinds they realized that they were not sailors and had no way to return back to the mainland. And as they discussed what would happen and decided to let the winds decide their fate; a ship, a familiar ship coasted their way. Gurney had returned.

At first it seemed like fate had responded but when Gurney revealed the true story they were left a little disappointed. Calwin had stored an arvic message of sound along with some valuable items and left these in Gurney's cabin. The sound memo said that Khan and Griz may not have died as Thryn had stated and would need the services of Falinquistamod. Gurney would have even considered it for free since he liked the wind follower but took the items as a bonus. Zorn had its use. Since then he had been scouring the oceans in the hopes of finding his former friends. Well, in truth, he always scours the oceans when not employed.

As they neared the urba, Khan was reminded of some pain in his neck and the wrongs that were done to him and his friend, too many wrongs. Thryn had stolen his Calwin; she had stolen his corius: both of them had stolen his life. Thieves they were. Not the thieves that steal items of monetary value, but real thieves that take what cannot be replaced or repaired and they did not care nor realize their thievery; and Khan would make sure that these thieves would not steal again so easily. Calwin could be spared but Thryn, at the very least, would have to make amends. And Griz, though he did not say so much in words, inside a noxy fire rose and he would have his revenge.

For Griz, revenge wasn't just a goal, it was a penetrating hunger that needed to be fed with the sprayed milk from the dying. Having milk splashed upon his armor, his face, reminded him that he was still breathing, reminded him that he was still needed, reminded him that there was hope in the absolution of life.